TALE

OF

"*Jeannette*"

AYSA FLOREZ

www.trafford.com

North America & international
toll-free: 1 888 232 4444 (USA & Canada)
fax: 812 355 4082

I dedicate this Play to my mother - Ester, who has passed away during the publication of the book.

CHARACTERS

MATHIES...Sacked, becomes a sailor

MARISOL.................................... young woman in the Amazon

ISABÈL.. Mathias's wife

ANDRÉ.. Loader, P.A. to the Navigator

SOFIA ....Gypsy Lady, Fortune-teller

FERDINAND.................................... Midshipman on 'Jeannette'

TIJUANA..Owner of the bar

CHARLES .... Seaman on the English ship

THE EXTRAS

FELIPE - a Cabin Boy on the ship "Jeannette"

FRANCOIS – the Ship's "Jeannette" Captain

RENAUD - the superior at the factory in France.

Molière - owner from whom the Marceau leasing a house

FRYER - accountant, hides in the closet be Gay.

CARLOS – the ship's "Jeannette" doctor.

LORETTA LENORA – two old rich ladies. The first appeals adore her cat. And they're neighbor with the Marceau's.

NARRATOR - is a male's voice from OFFSTAGE.

FIFI – a cat appears and belongs to madam Loretta. It's going to be killed as the play proceeds.

RETAILER #1 RETAILER #2 – they're seen in Act I, Scene 6.

YOUNG GYPSY – Roma woman appears in Act 1, at scene on the Marketplace.

DRAG QUEEN – A Gay man, and is called himself - Veronica. His real name is Paul; and he comes out from the closet, as story progresses. He is going to be killed in finale.

BENITO MACHADO - is the Governor in South America.

REPORTER – from a English newspaper

GIRLS - in the Bar; and at Night Club "Tijuana".

SETTINGS

Renaud Factory's office

Ferdinand's ship deck; and in a cubicle

Tijuana's club - resembled to a Night Club

Marisol's back yard

STAGING

This Play has not been staged as yet.

PART I: SCENE 1 - Onset of action happens in small-town, at Southern France.

SCENE 2: In the center of stage is extension in the form of a self-constructed house. Inside some parts of the furniture are kept. Here is the factory's office with waterfront view on the Sea, seen as people spinning in their chairs. Two of those are dressed in overalls, the men wearing suits, carrying papers. And those women are in dark skirts plus jackets.

ACT II SCENE 1 - On the stage decoration is a fragment of the mast; a small outbuilding in the form of ship that, also serves as the ship's upper deck.

At the back of stage is half-empty. Then the stage is well lit; lights are fallen on the emerged Renaud, who stood, looking in a displayed window. On other side of the stage is emerging Fryer that walks into the office.

SCENE 4 - The stage well lit: where change of attributes, and preparing the scene with movements.

At back of the stage see fragments of a ship in the Port. In a close proximity is an office, where hangs a map on role-playing wall; table furnished with bottles; and three chairs.

There in saw people are spinning a couple dressed in work overalls. Employees carry papers, men are dressed in suits and ties, women in a dark skirts and jackets.

Seen an office either of the factory with a waterfront view on the Sea.

SCENE 4 - Personifying in the stage far corner, added a phenomenon image of the landscape it's the Tropical Edge, where view of the Amazon area in the Rainforest.

SCENE 6 – Is hearing melody played by someone on a piano accordion.

PART II Act I – Scene: On stage is change of attributes for anew scenery, where are seen crowds presenting their products.

Scene 4 – The guitar player turns loud, and passionately strums the chords on a guitar is drowning, but creaking this gramophone. Hearing the boom of a drum is flattering to those beat, in the rhythm of South American dances, singing melody.

Scene 6 - With the first sounds of music sounds of music develops of unhurried procession of those, who active dancing ensue, as they perform intricate Pirouettes.

Scene 8: It'd execute grotesque of colorful performances, predicts fate of the hero, and sound tracks?

*Here is colorful scenery to be seen here: picture on the Market, use of fun at the Carnival Song-Dance performers. That acrobat amidst flying gymnasts, magician-fakirs, and synchronously here - is a torch with fire in the Circus.

PART II - Scene 1 On the stage is a small extension in the form of a ship. While in the background we can see fragments of ship's deck. There is the pyramid and guns, a rope, with flags from foreign countries, as well.

Scene 2: On the stage change of attributes on scenery where a hard rebuild, and preparing for the next picture: in a tent. On the stage decoration is a fragment of the mast; a small outbuilding in the form of ship that, also serves as the ship's upper deck.

SCENE 4, page 63 - On the stage change of attributes on scenery where a hard rebuild, and preparing for the next picture: in a tent.

On the stage decoration is a fragment of the mast; a small outbuilding in the form of ship that, also serves as the ship's upper deck.

PART III: There's metropolis of a modern city. Be heard noise in the street. The rustle of tires on the machines; grinding of the brakes be made noise.

And the scene, reconstructed in style Shop-design and business, mid-20th-century. A handcar, buses. Crowd is dancing (Ballet Ensembles and vocals). Active movements. Burning eyes, with arrival of those youthful nice bodies. Super-cafes and shops in the last century amidst visual of the city. Full of energy, rhythms, lovely music, has praised the English-style with ecstasy by youth: white and dark-skin persons, at 1920's, or early 1930's in the XX-Century.

PART III - Act 3 – in scene are disguised dressed in the form of the English Sailors, appear on stage: that group goes, eyeing around; on the go, alive by reading on tops from buildings, there are inscriptions in English. The scene well lit the as bright floodlights, and lighting the way appeared on the stage of the new English sailors.

PRODUCTION NOTES CONTENT:

A kaleidoscope of musical and song order, plastic, for Ballet picture with colorful lighting. It's presentation: POPURI of anthology by contemporary Pop or ROCK music.

The play is divided in three to four stages: the opening is taken place in a Factory's office. Next the actions move to a fragment in the form of a vessel. Partway sound of a lively melody can be heard offstage; along with guitar, and piano accordion received. At some point of the play dim lights emerge. There are.

TIME: period late 1920's, or 1930's, in the first quarter of XX-Century; during the Great Economic Depression.

PLACE: it begins in the Southern province of France. Then it moves to the Amazon, and continues in South America.

The information is focused here to help the readers to understand the Structure, and to enjoy the story.

ENSEMBLE:

There are **14** actors overall who have to be partaking in the Play/Musical.

Production notes go when the play is staged.

ACKNOWLEDGEMENTS

The author would like to thank various people for their support and encouragement.

PROLOGUE

NARRATOR (OFFSTAGE)

The story tells about what had taken place in difficult times, when the World was shaken by the crisis of Great Depression. Back then, many countries have been swallowed by unemployment; with countless of it's citizens sacked from their jobs. But the innocent people lost primarily their last savings. Neither wisdom, nor prudence, or diligent efforts by hard work have helped them; not even prayers eased. Au contraire, a recipe for disaster has brought in their hearts such fear to lose income that, brother would deceive his brother; and husband the wife with his children. More incredible thing ensue that mothers and fathers avoided open up the truth about they're earnings to their children, or help them else!

PART ONE

SCENE 1.

Here see a factory's office; there are people spinning in

their chairs.

On the back of the stage is Renaud - superior in the factory - when glances at an accountant named Fryer, who gives him business papers; he then instantly goes away.

View the back of stage is half-empty. Seen the stage well lit, and lights are fallen on the emerged Renaud, who stood, and looking in a displayed window. On the other side is emerging Fryer, who's walking into the Office.

FRYER
(Holds papers in his hands.)
Excuse, sir, I prepared for you the financial report?

RENAUD
(Looks at him.)
Who are you? Do you work on this plant?

FRYER
(His look of being scared.)
My name is Fryer, Mr. Renaud! And I work as an account, here! My dynasty had connection amid the Royal family and with Prince Philip, particular.

RENAUD

Really?

FRYER

Yes, that's a fact, sir!

RENAUD

Interesting! Is your name Fryer?

PAUSE. Fryer ducks his head. Next he has a word to say.

FRYER

Yes! As I said, my family was acquainted with Prince Philip! And, yes! Yes! Yes, my daddy was the Hitler! No! No! No, my mom - was not a Jew!

Fryer presents to Renaud business papers; and walks off.

He then runs, is passing Mathias, this last one appears here, and him being laughing on the way.

Mathias knocks at the door; then awkwardly stops at the door. He crossed the verge of an office, but is unstable seen he's foot-to-foot.

MATHIAS

Did you call for me, Master Chief?

RENAUD

How something like this happen in the world? Tough times began that, have brought dilemmas in society?

He sees at last Mathias, who stood near the door, and is looking awkwardly.

RENAUD

Oh, it's you? Yes, come in! Sit down over there. I'm sorry I forgot your name, man?

PAUSE. Renaud shows his finger down to a chair. He does not hear Mathias's schmooze, which is too nervous.

MATHIAS

Thank you, Mister Renaud! I'm Mathias Marceau!

Renaud is shamed; bows his head to look at the documents.

RENAUD

(He calms down.)
Yes, Marceau! How long have you been working in this factory?

MATHIAS

(Talks with pride, head high.)
Well, I came to the plant from the time, when I was eighteen years! Since then I have worked hard in here, Mister Renaud! Why are you asking me all these?

Renaud lowers his head to re-view papers, is looking into the void tensely. He lifts his head to look at Mathias.

RENAUD

Marceau, hard times fallen on our plant? It has led to problems elsewhere, due to Great Depression! In the light of this, I have to sack some of the staffs? I'm by now making a list of who will be sacked?

(PAUSE.)

RENAUD

That's why you were called here, because I'm planning in advance to controlling, but not so sudden to all of you're who to be dismissed?

MATHIAS
(His look changed - to grim.)
Mister Renaud, I was working a long time on plant with no liabilities...

(PAUSE.)

The main thing here is, that my wife is expecting a third baby. How can I support my family? If you're going to dismiss me? Please, Mister Renaud, have pity on us?

Matt falls silent; it looks if he was lost at sea. Renaud instead is uninterested with ridicule; and he is raising an issue. He produced a smile; as his voice is smooth.

RENAUD

Marceau, you're not alone in this hard situation! We all must overcome obstacles, be caused by Great Depression that is tied too a damn Economic crisis?

(PAUSE.)

As you see I just simply cannot help you? I am sorry, man!

Renaud stops. Next he is continuing in agitated voice.

RENAUD

Besides, why starting a third child? If you knew well that, you could not feed your family, specially the kids?

He stops short; takes gulps of air; becomes calm cool and collected. He changes talk with a twist of uncertainty.

RENAUD

Look, man, it has not been decided yet? If we're agreeing to sack all staffs or some? You'll be informed, in case, if you know what I mean?

Renaud became bored; so he lows his head to look at wristwatch. Mathias's altered to be upset. (PAUSE.)

RENAUD

Now, go back to work and do not waste my time?

SCENE 2.

In the center of stage is a self-constructed house. Inner some parts of the furniture are kept. On the table sit two kids are in the age of nine to twelve years; and plates with food set before them. The broods are eating. Here appears a woman, ISABÈL - mother of those broods, is rotating, and serving them.

She is putting food and a jug on the table in front of them. The children ate quietly; echo is heard from tapping of their spoons over iron plates.

ISABÈL

(Says in a gentle voice.)
Come on, kids, eat it! Don't you agree the food taste well?

KIDS IN UNISON
Yes! Thank you, mama!

Suddenly the front door opens, there enters Mathias, and at once is taken off topcoat, then hangs it on a hanger.

Next he removes his boots. The kids turn their heads, and saw their father; they're become excited; following the kids in unison are asking.

KIDS IN UNISON
Dad, what did you bring us?

Matt removes candies from his pocket, places them on the table.

MATHIAS
I've carried candies on the sticks.

Those broods get up of their sits are trying to grab one each of the candies, then waves his hands as he sings.

MATHIAS
(Shakes his head.)
No! Don't even think about! And, do not touch the sweets, better eat your Lunch, children! You'll have candies afterwards!

MATHIAS slowly came within reach of his wife, ISABÈL, who looks into his eyes curiously, but lovingly. She puts her hand up onto his shoulders; she then is asking him over.

ISABÈL
Darling, why you are not happy? Has something happened?

Mathias slants his head towards aside, as he's facial expressions and the eyes given her a warning to shut up.

MATHIAS
(He is half-whispering.)
Never mind, I'll tell you later.

Here ISABÈL that looks as if she is confused; and changed the pace of their conversation at once.

ISABÈL
Matt, are you going to eat?

Matt lowers his head, shakes with it, as he is reacting.

MATHIAS
(He's voice restricted.)
No, I do not want any food! For it'll be stuck down my throat, or climb it?

He takes a deep breath; is looking Isabel in the eyes, while she speaks out. She merrily slants her head to, where her kids sit, and declares in a tender voice.

ISABÈL
My darling, don't grieve. Matt, sit down and eat with the kids. They always glad to be in your company!

(PAUSE.)

Mathias, you're a great family man! Do you want, something to eat?

She became intrigued, and listens to Matt, whilst they're having tête-à-tête. Hearing his news, Isabel says softly, serious voice.

ISABÈL

Now, tell me, what's really happen to you? Were you a victim?

Matt's voice, on the contrary growing to be irritating.

MATHIAS

No, but today at work, I've got a warning of widespread layoffs! I'll be probably first to become jobless?

(PAUSE.)

After all, I was clearly explained by our Bosses that, we're waiting for the birth of our third child?

ISABÈL

And yet, your Boss did not want to understand how hard our situation is? Is that what you tried to say?

MATHIAS
(Covers his ears with hands.)
I did indeed! Would my ears better not hear it? And my eyes would not see it?

Mathias rotates; and waves a hand hopelessly. Next he moves to the bedroom, where his children slept. Waiting a bit, Matt listens warily. Ensuing he puts a finger to his lips; he gives a sign to be quite.

MATHIAS
Shush!

Upon returning, his attitude is changed to amusing. MATT waves a hand, when is talking with ISABÈL.

MATHIAS
(Talks in a half-whisper.)
On the way home I saw an old Buddy of mine,
André. Whatever ensued, he'll help me to get hired
as a Stevedore, in Port! What do you think, Isabel'?

She seems is sad; her head with a nervous twist from right-to-left;
but she talks softly, but anxiously.

ISABÈL
Matt, I would not like to see you working long
hours? Also, it's a hard job! But if you have no other
options? In that case let it be.

Mathias interrupts her; and is immediately re-joining.

MATHIAS
Here I'm, he said. I'm still concede, about him
asking, if I can knock up few hours at the night
shifts? He stops; takes a deep breath; and prolongs.

(PAUSE.)

Given, in the Port they I'll get paid roughly the
same there, than I have been working at the factory?

Her face alters - to be blissful with a sign of support.

ISABÈL
Well, if that is true, Matt? This idea
would not be so bad for you, after all?

(PAUSE.)

Then it's important for you to keep your new job!
As for the old job at the plant...

Pause. They stood and are looking at each other, as their shoulder move up and down.

SCENE 3.

Here appears the owner of this house - Molière, from whom Marceau's family leasing the property; but that house lacks of having a better habituation in.

Molière enters the house quietly; by removing his hat, and on the go he is snooping, and says in mockery.

MOLIERE
Well, ladies and gents, how are you? I have not seen you're all for a while! Is everything working in your family?

Mathias looks oddly at Isabel, when he is responding.

MATHIAS
Yes, we have all under control, Mister Molière! Thanks for asking, but we are all good! Why are you asking?

Molière is slightly tilted his bulky body to both.

MOLIERE
Yes! A rumor has it that you'll soon lose your job, on the plant, Mathias?

PAUSE. He stops; looks at them; takes breaths; and tells.

MOLIERE
If it's true, how do you fellows, Ought to pay for the house?

Mathias gazes at Isabel, they're seeming are lost at sea.

MATHIAS

Mister Molière, who told you that, Gossip? It's not
yet in definite, if I'll be dismissed from my job?

MOLIERE

That's what you say, but who knows? As peopled
would say: 'There is no smoke, without a fire'?

He spins, is facing Isabel, and he attends utterly her.

MOLIERE

Don't you agree, madam? That's why I came in
here, to remind you that, you cannot pay annually,
for the rent?

PAUSE. He stops talking; takes breaths, and is prolonged.

MOLIERE

The whole thing is to blame for that cursed Great
Depression? With it's economic crisis?

MATHIAS

As you can see my wife's expecting a baby? Sir, my
other kids are little? We don't need to be hassled?
And yet, Mister Molière, don't worry, if I lose my
job? I'll not allow my family to wander around!

———◆◆◆◆———

Now is variation of the scenery: seen a half-empty stage, where's
hanged a heavy curtains, covering the light dark blue - image of the
night, and a full moon there.

Here appears Mathias is carrying on his shoulders a sack. Following him is a man, André, who slightly breathless; has wore working overalls; him can be seen pickups bag.

ANDRÉ

Whoa, Matt? This is not fair? I spoke today to our casual loader, who told me an interesting story? He said that, couldn't wait until he will be dismissed from his job?

PAUSE. André stops briefly; looks around; takes a deep breath, and he prolongs telling.

ANDRÉ

And yet, Felipe has got hired to swim on the ship, abroad!

André does stop. He is rubbing one hand with his other.

ANDRÉ

There he's already given Sailor's uniform! Also, every day he gets food ration. Tomorrow is his last shift as a loader. It looks up, how this youngster gets on?

MATHIAS
(Awkward looks.)
André, are you sure about it? Maybe he fooled you around, so as to show off, before you?

ANDRÉ
(His look as if is uncertain.)
No, way! He would not lie! Felipe was sacked! His co-worker informed me, or do you think otherwise, Matt?

MATT picks up a heavy sack, recaps it on his shoulders.

MATHIAS

Well, André, can I say why not? I will come back tomorrow in the Port, and ask around it?

ANDRÉ

Okay! Now, don't stop, Matt! Keep on working! We need to finish unloading those sacks? Matt, get move it fast! 'Heels in hands and expand your steps'!

Both of the men walking off, and are leaving the stage.

SCENE 4.

Here its well lit, and at back of the stage see fragments of a ship in the Port. In a close proximity is an office, where hangs a map on role-playing wall; table furnished with bottles; and three chairs.

Captain of the ship, Francois appears be seated. Next to him the ship's Doctor - Carlos, and both sit around the table; they're taken some papers, and having begun to carefully review it.

Here Matt arrives, but he's look is awkward. Now, can be seen that, he captivated in his thoughts. Mathias turns to face the audiences, and starts addressing them.

MATHIAS

(Whispers to himself.)

I do not know why I came here? But my conversation with André has intrigued me? And yet, it fuelled me?

At the same time two men's heads up, as they're Francois and Carlos, ship's doctor; both are watching Matt's eyes.

The ship's Captain, Francois broke in Matt's thoughtful, says-on-line, and is referring to him, like orders him.

FRANCOIS
(Says strictly and loud.)
Hey, how did you get here? Who are you?

CARLOS
What can do we for you, mister?

MATHIAS
(He pulls up his head; talks to them.)
I'm sorry, gentlemen! I was advised by someone, to ask around?…

PAUSE. Matt clams up; inhales; and prolongs telling.

MATHIAS
That if I would come in Port, somebody in charge,
will sign me up at once, so as to work in here?

Those men are looking oddly at each other; and both start laughing, as their facial expressions having mimics. After composing himself, Francois re-joins alone.

FRANCOIS
Listen, man, are you sure that, you come in the
right place? Or maybe you got lost?

Pause. Captain is silent; is observing Matt from top to toe. Next he is responds with uncertainly; as Francois crosses with a leg-on-leg; but is kept his head straight.

MATHIAS

I am Mathias Marceau! In the truth is told, I don't know? Someone guided me to speak with you are, because I'm looking for a permanent employment?

Matt stops short; looks with plead at them; and prolongs.

MATHIAS

I was born on the sea, and am still a good swimmer!

Francois looks in his eyes; is examining him. He then interrogates, as is fixed his eyes with a stare at Matt.

FRANCOIS

What is your name? This is first of all, before you ask us each a question charter that are needed to log in, señor!

Mathias reports back clearly, loudly like military man.

MATHIAS

I'm Mathias Marceau! And I'm Matt for short, is at your service, sir!

Conducted by initiative the ship's doctor is asked over.

CARLOS

Secondly, Marceau, what sort of job you're looking for? Here you can take service either as a sailor, or a ship fitter, norm?

Mathias crosses with a leg-on-leg, is hesitantly telling.

MATHIAS

Señor, I worked at the plant for many years! But I was sacked from the job? And yet, I'm hopeless, because I do not know, how to run a steamship, sir?

He stops; breathes deep; his look as if be lost in sea.

MATHIAS

I have a family with two children to feed! But soon we are expecting a third child to be born?

(PAUSE.)

Please, seniors, take in that I'm in a difficult fiscal situation! A bit more, and my children will have nothing to eat?

He stops short; it seems as him being gasping for air.

MATHIAS

In case, if you have got a permanent position, I'm begging you, seniors, hire me, please? As I am myself ready to fulfill any duties!

PAUSE. Now the Captain is taken the floor, and acting by stopping him.

FRANCOIS

We do cognize to your situation. Let's say, we accept you in the services? Then you'll have to swim aboard in the open Seas, and to be separated from your family and close friends more often, than not?

He stops talking; breathe in. Francois looks at Matt, and prolongs to tell more.

FRANCOIS
It's the first due! Secondly, you have to get consent and resolve with your wife, before make a decision?

He stops; looks at Matt; takes breaths, and he prolongs.

FRANCOIS
And yet, we in our turn need to know, who you are? Only then decide: if yes or not allow you serving on a freighter Ship? Now, do you have any questions?

MATHIAS
(He presages loudly.)
No, sir, everything is clear!

It's a setback for Mathias, while Francois is training him, and states clearly and loudly.

FRANCOIS
Wrong answer! Hear a correct reply that, you've to be retorting, Senior Captain of the fleet! Same stands – for señor Doctor! Did you understood what I mean, Marceau?

Matt stood with his Shoulders Square, he become eager.

MATHIAS
(Loudly.)
Yes, Captain!

Mathias is waving a hand up in the air; and prolongs.

MATHIAS
Sir, I want to sign up for that job, at once! I am sure my family would not mind me be absent it's not apt to be on a cruise forever, true?

Next those two men at the same time saying-so.

BOTH IN UNISON
Who knows? And yet, this is how it will turn out, to be?

Next the ship's doctor, ship's doctor declares alone.

CARLOS
Marceau, after you exit, next turn right. There you'll see a door, where the register office is. You must get recruited to become a member of our ship's crew! There you should receive travel papers, as a sailor. Also you will be given a daily rations. Once you filled out the forms, return it back in here! Also it's vital to bring A Medical Certificate from the doctor?

Resulting the ship's Captain, in his turn says-so.

FRANCOIS
It's all clear? Do you've any questions?

MATHIAS
No, sir! Can I've your OK to go?

By shaken their heads, means both are given consent.

BOTH IN UNISON
Yes, you can! You free to go!

Matt's eyebrows rose up from a surprise. As he has turned around, then quits the place, immediately.

SCENE 5.

There comes into view a house, where Mathias lives with his family. He slowly approaches the entrance. It's also visible he is into thoughts that are absent somewhere.

MATHIAS
(Talks to himself.)
What will I tell my wife? She's going to give birth soon? I have no other options? I was sacked from the plant!

MATHIAS
(PAUSE.)
And yet, the living is too costly, because we must manage somehow to pay for housing?

Unexpectedly Isabel comes from behind to Matt; and hugs his shoulders. She puts her head on his back. Isabel's a sudden outburst has scared him; seen his shoulders are slightly trembling.

MATHIAS
Isabel, you have got me a bit scared. More so, don't do it again?

He stops talking; settles down; and he is continuing.

MATHIAS
It's good to have you with me! I'm missing only the Children, where are they?

Isabel looks with affection; says in a loving voice.

ISABÈL

I m sorry, dear! I just wanted the children to…

Isabel tails off instantly, as she seems being upset.

ISABÈL

They're playing in the street. You want me to call them to come home?

Matt glances over, and has pointed to a chair for her to sit down. He then breathes deeply, and talks seriously.

MATHIAS

Not, yet! Isabel, I want to talk to you alone! Someone is praised me, and today I went to see a place. There I have arranged and secured a stable job, where I'll start working soon!

He stops; looks at her, takes breathe; and is prolongs.

MATHIAS

But, I don't know how you, Isabel and the children will deal with it?

Isabel pays attention; smiles, as if she's blooming with.

ISABÈL

Mathias, what sort of work as such that you've found it so soon?

Mathias makes a deep outbreak; and he says-so, is rashly.

MATHIAS

Isabel, you know something, in these days and my
age, it's hard to find a decent job? Besides, I'm not a
teen anymore! I do not get many options for a any
jobs, specially in our region?

He stops taking; looks at her, and takes breaths.

MATHIAS

Today I walked into the port and was employed
there as a Sailor on the ship "Jeannette"! This way
I'll be sailing to foreign countries!

He is keen; but Isabel postponed thumbprint, as the expression of
her face altered - to pallor.

Raising her arms, Isabel puts them up on chest cross-prayer, her
voice being trembling with a respond. Seen how the blood rushing
to her cheeks, tears is rolling down her face.

ISABÈL

Matt, why are you doing it to us? Was it not any
other vacancy there? You have not even been sacked
from the plant yet? In be said that, what should I
do? I am giving birth in a month or two? What
about our children? Who will take care of them,
when I go in labor?

Mathias in a slightly irritating voice, laid-back, as is waving his
hands.

MATHIAS

Isabel, why do you not agree that we live in
province where is a small chance finding a job? In
my case I would either sweat as a loader? Or I'll go
sailing, it was no other vacancy then and there?

Matt stops; takes a deep breathe; and he is continuing.

MATHIAS

I have always dreamed to be sailing! With marrying you, I never fulfilled my dreams!

Matt discontinues; takes a deep breathe; and he prolongs.

MATHIAS

A ship is sailing abroad soon. For all I know we might come back before the due of birth of our baby?

Isabel is crying; while observes the entreaty, tears have froze in her eyes.

ISABÈL

I am sorry, dear! You never talked of your dreams?

PAUSE. Mathias's head is leaning sideways; as his voice is slightly demanding.

MATHIAS

You never asked me! By the way in Port, I was given a food rations. I'll get provisions daily with all that you need for yourself and the children, up till departure of the ship. When I go sailing, every time you come to the port you will receive help for everything you must have!

Mathias puts a parcel on the table. When he opened the parcel, inside it's turned out to be some sort of food and fruits. Seen Isabel is given an uneasily smile.

ISABÈL
(Says in a shaky, but soft voice.)
Matt, if you've already decided? Then, why don't you go sailing? I'll not stay in your way?

She stops short; is breathing deeply; and prolongs.

ISABÈL
Just if you promise to return home from the voyage, before I will give birth? Can you, Matt?

He does not listen to her response; while kept talking.

MATHIAS
Maybe I can? Did you make lunch?

She ducks her head, like: 'Okays'. Matt then prolongs.

MATHIAS
Now, it's important to call the kids, Here? I want to eat alongside them!

LIGHT OUT.

SCENE 6.

Here is showing, these crowds presenting their products. With the first sounds of music sounds of music develops of unhurried procession of those, who active dancing are succeed, as they perform intricate Pirouettes. Sunshades visible. There're selling books, utensils, clothing, food, and more.

Now appears Matt, who walks alongside his family. They're walking desperately back and forth, amid masses; one stop at each counter charmingly; next by anew kiosk.

MATHIAS
(Declares loudly to his family.)
Let's go ahead do not stop! Or we can get lost! The fair occupies huge area where it's easy to get lost in the crowd?

Seen, these buyers are, next a man shouts in an accent?

RETAILER #1
Good people! Do not pass by! Come on down! Your trip is to buy it! I give up stuff, all for nothing!

His nationality - Magyar, and the owner of a tent dress, Bandera, those hatch from its tray. He is waving things, while in a gaming voice, at the same time, emphasizes.

RETAILER #2
Quickly! Buy plenty that you can grab it, even what does not exist!

Now come into view the ladies that are seen Loretta with a kitty-cat, Fifi.

Next to her is a Superior Lenora; those two are neighbors with Marceau's family. Loretta is caressing a cat's skin. The cat, meanwhile, is conveniently fits up on Loretta's arms; and at that moment she says-so.

LORETTA
Fifi did not sleep last night, and I sang her a lullaby! I do not know, what is to think? Could Fifi

LORETTA

fell ill? What do you think, Lena, must I call to her
a Doctor?

Observing around, Lenora pick up pieces, in a calm voice

LENORA

Loretta, dear, I don't even know, what to advice
you? Have you or anyone over fed Fifi, that's why
her stomach has ached?

PAUSE. Loretta reacting by a surprise - is petting a cat.

LORETTA

What did you say? I'm following Fifi diet. My
husband does not intrude. Do not even joke about
it, Lena, I Buy the freshest food directly from The
market! Is it not so, Fifi?

Lenora puts a smile; as noticing in the crowd Marceau's family; and
she pokes a finger in the direction of them.

LENORA

Loretta, look over there! I glimpse now Marceau's
family amid the crowd?

LORETTA

Where? I don't see them? What are they also came
to this Fair?
(PAUSE.)

LORETTA

Wow! It's a shocker? What are they doing here?
Where are they? I can't see them, anywhere?

Loretta turns to look around, peers into the crowd. She shows a finger towards the Marceau's family.

LENORA

Look, Lora, they're over there!

PAUSE. Then and there she pokes a finger toward them.

LENORA

Lori, look out to your right in the crowd? Can you see them, now?

As she peers, and notices them; then her face turns with facial expressions of surprise.

LORETTA

Oh, yes! Now I can see them! One would think they have money to spend at the fair? From what I've heard, they're barely made ends meet? Too rich for me there? Come on, let's walk up to them, and probe? What's your view on it, Lena?

She nods as a sign of consent; when tilts her head aside.

LENORA

Okay, Lori! Let's go then, and talk to them? But, you'll inquire alone!

Those ladies make their way with struggle; pushing people on the way, and moving on in the four of Marceau. Once the ladies approached Marceau's. Loretta began probing all of the Marceau; hearing her speech with overturns; but, on her face is visible a malicious smile.

LORETTA

Madame and Mr. Marceau! We are welcoming you all! How are you?

PAUSE. Matt smiles, and is re-joined openly, but timidly.

MATHIAS

Good day, Madame Loretta! And to you too, Madame Lenora! How you are both doing?

WOMEN IN CHORUS

Good morning, Mathias and Isabel! How are you? What's your family up to here? Buying things for the upcoming Newborn baby?

MATHIAS

Partly it is! Mrs. Loretta and you venerable, Madame Lenora! I have found a new job!

Loretta looks intrigued, and is asked with irony:

LORETTA

What's this job such as it good for you that can buy the whole Market?

MATHIAS

It's not quite true, my dear, ladies! We have not saved so much money. I will be serving as a sailor on the ship to navigate abroad?

PAUSE. Those women look at each other, are confused.

LORETTA

Really? What is so vital to have with you on that trip? Where are you sailing to, Mathias?

All became silent; are looking at each other. Isabel, picks up calmly, her voice is slightly shaken.

ISABÈL

You know something ladies, Matt is going to sail, soon! That's why our family came to the fair to buy a lot that will be essential for his trip!

ISABÈL stops talking; does a bow to look down at her stomach; and she's stroked it with a grin. (PAUSE.)

ISABÈL

Aside from it, we're buying here a great deal of stuff for our Future newborn! We hope it's a boy?

Catching her head that be slightly tilted; and she looks at him oddly.

LENORA

Its all be weird, Mathias? You worked on the plant for many years? Then what a change of scenery? You're sailing off and leave your family in such difficult situation?

He shakes his head; looks at his kids, and with faith.

MATHIAS

You've aforesaid my motive, madam to go sailing! in a bid to ensure the future for my family and kids' sake!

PAUSE. He stops short; takes breathes, and prolongs.

MATHIAS

If you have not heard yet, I was sacked from the plant, and I need a job! Since I was hired to be a sailor! How about I'll bring you a gift from abroad would you like that, Lady Lenora?

He then turns sideways to face Loretta, and tackles her.

MATHIAS

What about you, Madame, Loretta! What sort of gifts you're wishing?

Loretta gazes with wonder; her eyes widened, her mouth is half-opened.

LORETTA

Mathias, are you really sailing?

Matt nods his head, in accord. Lenora takes the floor: looks with wonder, her shoulder slightly up are moving.

LENORA

If that is true, then you, Mathias, bring me from abroad most exquisite shawl! So that, I can wear it on all festivities?

Loretta, meanwhile, looks be puzzled; has a squeaky little voice; tilts her head aside, and she's implying.

LORETTA

For me, dear Mathias, you bring me the most fashionable rags for my adored Fifi! Okay?

PAUSE. Next she is rotated, and asked over.

LORETTA

Isabel, dear, can we talk to you in private? Let's us move out, my dear, to the sideways?

Isabel amidst the children, next Lenora and Loretta with a cat in her arms jointly they are eager to talk; without waiting for approval, those women go off toward aside - behind the scenes.

———◆→)◆(←◆———

SCENE 8.

On the stage appears a band of those Gypsies that are drawing attention of the folks on the fair. Mathias is searched the area, as he turns around.

Suddenly, he is noticed a group of Gypsies approached him; and he is inspired by execution of Gypsy Group singing and dancing.

As notion that drew the attention to an old woman, who has for a long time watched methodically him, Matt felt upon his skin-convulsed goose bumps, as if the lady is staring straight through his soul.

Instantly another woman, this time a young Gypsy, runs up to Matt, and is offering services of the Fortune telling.

This young Gypsy lady tries to convince, and indicating through her hands, but she is laughing into his eyes.

Mathias felt upon his skin convulsed goose bumps, as if Gypsy, staring straight through his soul.

Then another woman a young Gypsy, runs up to Matt, and is offering of the Fortune telling. The Gypsy lady phonates the words intone, indicates to her hands; as is laughing in his eyes, she does speak with an accent, and intones.

YOUNG GYPSY

Hey, handsome man! Put coins in my hand, and I'll tell you your Fortune: what was, and what awaits for you in the future?

PAUSE. Matt pushes her hand away, when reacts angrily.

MATHIAS

No, thanks! I know you Roma people are skillful on having taken money from us, and deceiving others? As for me, I have no desire for a Penny Wishes! Be a Con Artist, you go over there and trick those with pockets full of cash! Gypsy Lady, do you mind? Cause I'm myself too capable to put on tricks...

Matt doesn't have time to retreat upon her approach, when this same woman, stared at him aside, and came within reach of him. Her look is of elderly, and was christened Sofia. The lady stares into Matt's eyes; and suddenly she grabs his sleeve, like being given him a sign of warning.

Mathias turns to look back; but is said in a tone that is rude to this old Gypsy: except, he's stared at that group with a weird look, and says loud in an irritating voice.

MATHIAS

Hey you, woman? I said I have no money! Beside, I do not need a Fortune Telling!

He stops talking; rotates, and nods to the bare back of the crowds.

MATHIAS

You better go to those rich men with they're thick wallets, cause I do not wish to hear a lie, no way!

Yet Mathias tries to escape, but Sofia keeps his sleeve grasped. She instead pronounces the words also with an accent, and by closely looking into his eyes.

SOFIA

You're in vain towards me! I've faced a great deal of risks in life, but my Word is not a lie! Why would I put my reputation on the line? Many of honest folks trust my Fortune Telling, and I don't deceive them! It's how I earn my bread! I can see what waits for them in the future, gift of a hook up that will please them, as me evenly earn pennies? No way I would lie!

She stops short; takes a deep breath, and prolongs.

SOFIA

I spent years learning to predict people's fate? And for you, my dear Falcon, now is what you should know: before I tell you your name starts with the letter "M"…

But Matt is broke it; laughs in her eyes; and speaks out.

MATHIAS

Well, you surprised me, lady? Your Roma people in the world are full of scams. A fable of how smoothly you all make up a story? Even we, common people have not been that clever to been aware of? In case if words wrong, you invent new…

Sofia is with a piercing look, as she dugs into his eyes.

Mathias imagined, like if soil slide has left from under his feet; even he feels goose bum ran over his body. He then also began hearing echoes of his own voice?

SOFIA
(Be heard audacity in her voice.)
That's enough of abuse! Now you shut up! Mathias,
listen carefully what I'm intent to tell you?

She points a finger up to her mouth, like keep quite.

SOFIA
Mathias, you were christened with this name! Am I
wrong that told you?

A sudden he has felt as if chained to the place, and cannot move
around, like magic had him glued.

MATHIAS
You're not mistaken, Gypsy lady! Who told you that?

PAUSE. He restrains himself; talks in a calm voices.

MATHIAS
Forgive me! How can I call you?

This Gypsy lady has fixed her eyes, when said her name.

SOFIA
I am, Sofia! Now, listen carefully, Mathias, I have
to tell about your future? You aware good enough
of your own past! Now, do you wish to hear about
mystery of your future? And if do you wish me to
tell you of your fate, or not?

He remains at a position of mysticism, as if be drunk; it only hears
her voice.

MATHIAS
Welcome, Gypsy lady! Okay, tell the whole truth, what awaits for me in the future?

Sofia is pronouncing words like gave meaning, and she looks into his eyes.

SOFIA
So, Mathias, do you're preparing to travel far? But you won't go by train, not riding on a horse back? Instead you're sailing on the ship, abroad! Far from your family and children. In to isolated terra, where tests awaits you with trivia, compare to the suffering that will be inflicted on you, in someplace!

———◆➤❉◄◆———

Mathias laughs; gazes with wonder; as is trying to turn his head, but not in force.

MATHIAS
And what is special about for me over there, abroad? Will I, or not become rich, straightaway?

Sofia talks in a sad voice, and her spell falls on him.

SOFIA
No, sweetheart! You won't be rich! Instead you're going to learn about Human love? And yet it will not please you! For that Love won't bring you any Happiness, except for - punishment!

PAUSE. She stops short; breathes deeply, and prolongs.

SOFIA

As for the newborn, your son: he must be named
Mathias, in memory of you, Because you, Falcon,
will not return home alive? If you decide to sail on

SOFIA

the Ship far off! Though you'll be buried elsewhere,
but not in homeland!

Isabel' came and interrupts; looks with fear; a nervous laugh; and
she tags the Gypsy lady by her sleeve.

ISABÈL

Hey, you, Gypsy lady - I spit on your prophecy!
What, my husband will not return? I'll be given
birth soon? And my children need their father! It's
your wicked foretelling? Thence Bite your tongue!
How I wish to spit on you three times! You get the
Hell out from us, as far, as possible!

PAUSE. She stops short, turns to Matt, and tackles him.

ISABÈL

Matt, do not listen to this Witch! As for you,
Gypsy lady, you will not get a penny from me!

Here is seen Isabel' drags Mathias away from Gypsy lady.

LIGHTS FADE.

SCENE 9.

Part of the stage is on extension in the form of a ship. In the stage's
background are seen fragments of the deck.

Now appears a crowd - one group is dressed in sailors uniform, another group worn civil clothing.

Those sailors are saying goodbyes to that crowd. There can see the people are flapping their hands in farewell, it's a sign that the ship is sailing off.

Matt is wearing the sailor's uniform. Here be seen that, he says goodbye to his family; when is referring to them.

MATHIAS
Well, today is the day for the ship's departure. And I leave you behind! How will you cope without me be by your side? What can become of you're all? Now a word of advice to you my daughter, help your mother!

PAUSE. Matt does a half-turn, and is saying to his son.

MATHIAS
As for you my son, be decent and, in the house-owner, instead of me. Do you understand me, son?

Isabel weeps, wipes tears from her eyes; grabs Matt for the waistcoat, how-to, but is not willing to let him go.

ISABÈL
Mathias, dear, you do write to me, often? And yet, you promised to come back in time?

Mathias looks be sad; as he responds with derision.

MATHIAS
Isabel, I'll try, but I do not know? When the voyage ends, but I'll not back in time? Yes, Isabel,

it can happen? And if you'll see it's time for you to give birth?…

Matt stops short; looks at her caring; as he prolongs.

MATHIAS

Even if I won't be here, when you're given birth to our son? Then I'm asking you, please, name our boy, Matthew? That's upon me coming home, whereas he knew, whom his father is?

LIGHTS UP ON:

In the background is a picture: seacoast, where Loretta that strolls with her cat. Stopping, she peers into the crowd, where notices Mathias is among the people, is saying goodbye to his family. Loretta then lifts a hand, and is begun waving it in their direction.

Right then the cat suddenly is pulled out off her hand; jumps down on the ground; and it runs away - offstage. Loretta shouts, is edgily looking around, and she sobs.

LORETTA

Help, good people! Help to catch, Fifi! Somebody, give me back my Cat, please! No, Fifi! Don't do it?

Suddenly is heard sound of wheels, of a retarding car.

———◆✦❈✦◆———

LIGHTS UP ON:

After a brief Blackout, at the stage appears André out there, in the port that occurs among them are saying goodbye, and the mass, as André appeals to the crowd.

ANDRÉ

Respectable, seniors and madam! To whom this cat belongs? Can you see, a Cat crossed the road, but it was hit by a car! Is any know, if this cat has the homeowner?

Loretta steps up in front as to claim Fifi; and says-so.

LORETTA

This is my Fifi! What's happen to it? Is she alive? I will not survive, if something...

ANDRÉ

Madam, your cat was hit by a car! I'm sorry, but it's befall dead instantly!

André passes a cat's corpse to Loretta; that she's aloud, but sorrowfully advises Loretta, who is crying; he keeps the cat up in her arms; be as a Madwoman shows of to all.

LORETTA

Madam and gentlemen, it's my Fifi! Look at her it was killed by a car! This is a bad sign, and - Karma!

Loretta indignantly turned to face the crowd. But, has not found support to her grief amid people. Seeing as she quits, as her cry is impulsively loud on the go.

CROWD IN CHORUS

(Are exclaiming.)
A fair wind for you, Seamen! And seven feet to you, under the keel!

From behind the stage, unexpectedly, a Gypsy lady wisely is looking at one in the crowd. Sofia brings her look, in the wake on cast off of the ship; where Mathias is there, standing on the upper deck of "Jeannette".

SOFIA

Who's in love it's become Soul free. But freedom is a threat to marriage! Meza a man with grey-eyes as might swan by the Sea? When the grey-eyed man has come miles in mutiny, where come miles in mutiny? There he'll get to know the girl be vandal!

PAUSE. Makes signs, as it seems she listens to somewhat from out space.

SOFIA

Amaze, she wins as is named Amazonian beauty! I hear more as the waves are beating over the Dreadful rocks! Maze the meeting will soon happen!

LIGHTS FADE.

ACT TWO.

SCENE 1

Here emerges the senior Navigator, Johnny. Pronto is the scenery of the mast, below-deck. In the upper corner of the stage, the audience sees the ship's Captain Francois.

Near stood doctor Carlos who is with a complacent smile, as his shoulders popped out of the ship's hold.

The Navigator, Johnny appears standing on deck, he turns his gaze to face the spectators. Closed eyes, his hands are hanging over forehead Johnny's hidden from a sunray, and he carefully peers into the distance of the Ocean.

In the center of the stage emerges Felipe, a cabin boy is cheerfully whistling to the tune, while he mops the deck. In upper left corner the midshipman, Ferdinand and Gerard - the Naval officer.

Is seen the first assistant, André. Light is directed a new picture at the white clouds, but no warnings of a Storm at sea. The Sun is in the zenith.

Suddenly, the Navigator, Johnny interrupts this whistling Felipe; rotates, and refers to Midshipman, Ferdinand with a strong point of view, his tone indicates, as he looks closely; is shoved a finger in his mouth, and puts it up in the air like he checks weather vane.

JOHNNY
From what I see, the wind is very impetuous, where clouds are gathering in the sky? How wicked I maybe sound, Midshipman, but my prediction that is going to be ghastly storm at the Sea!

The Midshipman looks oddly at Johnny; and says in doubts.

FERDINAND

Are you certain about it, Navigator?

JOHNNY

I think I am not mistaken here, señor!

PAUSE. He turns to face the Cabin boy. He then prolongs.

JOHNNY

Cabin boy, go and find the Naval Officer and assistant Ferdinand? Because the Captain have to be told of the situation that might occur?

CABIN BOY

Are you sure about it, Navigator? This cannot be endeavor? Look up in the sky is blue there's not a cloud?

JOHNNY

Put aside talking, Cabin boy! And do what's you told not fancy going in trouble to a battalion to combat?

CABIN BOY

No, sir! I'll report at once of your concern to first assistant of Midshipman and to the Captain?

Felipe runs up to a naval; there is André stood, whose hands indicating, as he explains to the sailors. Given Ferdinand is the first Assistant to the Navigator that mumbles; as they're aboveboard approached Johnny. However, pronto talks only the Midshipman, Ferdinand.

NAVAL GERARD

Why did you called on us, mate?

FERDINAND

Chief Navigator, we've to inform the Captain of your concern?

JOHNNY

(Picks up, and continual.)

You see, I was watching the sky, and so I think that a killer storm at the sea, is approaching us!

NAVAL GERARD

What's the problem, chief Navigator?

JOHNNY

Shouldn't we inform the Captain? So that Storm won't take us by a surprise?

NAVAL GERARD

(He rotates, is facing Felipe.)

In be said, now, Felipe, go down to the Captain's cabin, and tell him that we have a storm coming up! Did you get it, Cabin Boy?

CABIN BOY

Yes, señor, Naval officer!

JOHNNY

Then go down to his cabin, quickly?

CABIN BOY

I am already on my way, sir!

He quickly walks off, leaves behind the scenes.

LIGHTS UP ON:

The stage is filled with bottles on the ship desk, and 3 chairs as well. The ship's Captain, Francois dressed in naval uniform; close by is the ship's Doctor.

Meanwhile, Francois and Carlos sit down at a table, and began playing cards; they're immediately into gamble of bridge, or Poker. Here appears Felipe, who has quickly stepped in; he then turns to face the audience.

CABIN BOY

I am sorry, Captain and you too, Doctor! Allow me to report?

CAPTAIN

Report, sailor, what's the matter occurred that is so urgent?

CABIN BOY

Captain, and you Doctor! Senior Officer and chief Navigator ask me to report it could start a violent storm at Sea?

CAPTAIN

It's good to know before hand! Let the crew and Sailors know! As I'll be on the deck soon. Is that clear?

CABIN BOY

Yes, Captain, I'll warn the crew!

PAUSE. The Captain nods, as a sign of his consent.

CAPTAIN

Yes, you can! Thank you, Felipe! You may go, now!

A hand hung down over the temple, as the Cadets do it in honors; having turned round, he walked off.

LIGHTS UP ON:

After a brief Blackout - the scene well lit: where saw those two Sailors on the deck; and one that is leading the conversation amidst them is Mathias.

MATHIAS
(He's turned to face the man.)
Navigator, how do you know when a storm will hit?

JOHNNY
Sailor, I've had many years experience, to go in the swimming, and I can tell almost all treachery of the Sea and its Caprices!

PAUSE. He stops; a turn facing Matt, and is continuing.

JOHNNY
Let's talk about you, Matt, people said that, you were born on the Sea, or not?

MATHIAS
That's exactly right, chief Navigator! The sea is my passion! I have always dreamed to go sailing, but it was not easy to do so, either one thing would go in my way, or the other. Only now my dreams come true!

JOHNNY
Listen, Matt, only at first glance, it seems the Sea
dream adventure, but, no!

He stops; takes breaths; and prolongs with narrative.

JOHNNY
At times, the sea is quiet, and submissive! But,
there comes a point it can kill you! Waves can
reach eight meters height, remarkably, idem on
the bottom of the sea? If thou shalt not tough
enough and fear to stop yourself from be afraid to
deal with storms at Sea, then it's the end of you?
Understood? If you do can withstand danger? Then
you'll become a sailor!

———◆•×◆•●————

SCENE 2.

On the stage a fast change of scenery, symbolizing the Sea-storm:
grey clouds; sound of a gusty Wind howls, burst of lightning, and
a lot of attributes.

The stage well lit: visibility of a Storm symbolizes the swinging
Sail. Idem happens on the deck, where be seen - are couple of the
Sailors, and Mathias endure anti-wind.

MATHIAS
Midshipman, wind is too strong? I fear that I can
be thrown overboard?

JOHNNY
(Confidently.)
No fear, Sailor! Grab the ropes and hold on to it!

FELIPE

Matt, this is my first entry to the open Sea! But I've never been in such tough situation, even on shore?

JOHNNY

Sailors, throw to shoot the breeze its better if you in a mood to seize, the ropes! But don't snub, and keep up defying! It's hub by force of uneven hour? If not, you'll be thrown overboard! Then you can rattle, where to tattle, at what time find yourselves on the bottom of the sea?

SAILORS IN CHORUS

Yes, sir! We do exactly that! We will keep hold the ropes, strong!

———◆◆◆◆◆———

The Captain appears, and appeals towards the viewers.

CAPTAIN

(He is facing the sailors.)
How you're holding up, guys? Keeping up, yes?

SAILORS IN CHORUS

We're trying, señor Captain, to hold on to the ropes!

CAPTAIN

Stay closer one-to another, if the waves arrive it would be safer to keep the balance! Let's hold on stiff, then pull the ropes to you, as it's not miff! Times two: and go for it, Sailors!

LIGHTS UP ON:

After a brief blackout, change of scenery on the stage, and increasingly illumines the picture of the day there: where the Sun is shining.

Now appears Matt that is looking out to the viewers; his hangs up over-forehead, covering the eyes from light; and he is looking meticulously into a distance, where the Horizon mergers with the Ocean - into a single space.

As silence is broken, Matt rotates, and is asked Johnny.

CAPTAIN
Thanks a lot, Chief Navigator!

Johnny is smiling; flickers with a wink when he nods in the "OK" sign.

END OF PART 1.

PART TWO

SCENE 1.

Light falls into the Centre; where Felipe is mopping the mast of a ship. Hearing the Cabin boy is singing. On the back of the stage is visible Naval officer, Ferdinand. On the opposite side, is emerging a first assistant to the Navigator - André. Further, appears from offstage, skimming passing Johnny – the Chief Navigator of the ship "Jeannette". Here is heard a singing Cadet, Felipe on the mast of the ship.

FELIPE

> Through storm the waves have thrown us in the sea: to the right or to the left who knows, if only we can see? While our forms hold balance wide? We might in norm get revive, if after a storm we can survive? Amazing since it's weird for I means in to learn fasten up the ropes? I guess with coming home the Sailors miss the warm, and kiss those pretty girls! And yet, what Sailors miss the most is the Sea? Anew Appointment may be met for them to see?

------◆◆◆◆◆------

Johnny drew attention to the Hall; see his Palm hangs over-forehead, shielding his eyes, as he stares intently into a distance.

Mathias, sudden interrupts Felipe's song; then directly he is turning to the Captain.

MATHIAS
(He's bewildered.)
Captain, I can see the shore at a close distance?

CAPTAIN
That's how it is, Sailor! We are getting closer to the port, where the Tropical edge is a few miles from the River Amazon.

PAUSE. He stops short; and glances over those Sailors.

CAPTAIN
Sailors, listen to my command! All aboard! Sailors, get up on deck, and get ready to moor "Jeannette" to the river Banks of the Amazon!

Johnny has drawn to him; and turn to face the officers.

JOHNNY
Yes, Captain!

CAPTAIN
(Loudly, clearly meets jerky.)
As for the Navigator, we are only a dozen nautical miles from the main port! Now, assemble the crew up on the upper deck! And prepare to moor "Jeanette" to the river Banks? Get hold of the ropes!

THE NAVIGATOR
(Access it; and rotates towards the sailors.)
Yes, sir! Tars and crew, listen to Capitan's command! Now, all climb on the deck! Next all of you're from the crew to line up...

SAILORS IN CHORUS
Yes, Chief Navigator! All as one to get up on the deck!

THE NAVIGATOR
Raise the sails! And give the ship a full move!

SAILOR #1
Yes, to raise the sails!

SAILORS #2
Yes, sir, to raise the sails!

SAILOR #3
Yes, to raise the sails! There, get a full speed of the ship!

SAILORS IN CHORUS
The ship is to get a full move!

LIGHTS OUT.

NARRATOR
In the distant, where Tropical edge, in South America, where the ship "Jeannette" docked In's Bay, near to the Banks of Amazon River!

(PAUSE.)

Shortly after arrival of the vessel on shores a group of Sailors are having stepped out. And Mathias is also in the company with them on foot...

LIGHTS UP ON:

After a brief blackout, on stage change of scenery, which have highlighted: picture of the day - The Sun hovers. A Painting: personifying the Tropical Region of the Amazon.

In the upper corner of the scene, added a - scenery - the emergence of a landscape: a view of an Amazon's Forest.

TRANSITION TO:

SCENE 2.

On the stage change of scenery, hard covers: is a picture of the day. The Sun is soars. Now be shown painting - In the Tropics of the Amazon.

LIGHTS DIM.

———◆◆◆◆◆◆———

The Stage is well lit, where a change of scenery for: the Sailors appear, are walking slowly through the City's square of that Tropical edge.

Those Sailors also pass through other part of the city; and going as far off as downtown.

LIGHTS OUT.

———◆◆◆◆◆◆———

A change of scenery, the stage lights up again, where are seen those Sailors, and Mathias in the company goes along with them, is looking around, whenever they visit other places, where things go ahead for all.

Sudden the sailors have stopped, where saw from afar glance a tavern. Except the place resembled more to a bar, and it's called 'Flamingo'.

SAILOR #2
Hey, sailors! We have already bypassed central place in this town! Learn about trail that is leading to Rainforest of the Amazon?

ANDRÉ
(He talks as if is boring.)
Yes, so what? We learned it is the mouth of the Amazon River. We do not need a lecture. As we all in a favor to look for anew place? Where All-stars Amiable? What do you say to that, guys?

PAUSE. André nods his head to the bar, and is winking.

SAILORS IN CHORUS
That's a great idea, brother!

SAILOR #1
What about thou the new sailor, is it not your name, Matt?

Mathias has nodded his head, as a sign of 'Okay'.

ANDRÉ
Yes, it is! Matt are you coming with us? Or you afraid of your wife mate?

MATHIAS

I am not afraid of anyone! Of course, I will come with you're! For I've never been to such places as this, before?

The Sailors with a stare at him, next to each other; and they're begun laughing. See they're walking boldly into the Tavern, titled "Flamingo" - in backstage.

LIGHTS OUT.

SCENE 3.

The landlord of the bar, Louise de Santos, abruptly walks around, to be ensured there is order in. Here, the host bar is a place, where counter with an old gramophone, as landlord puts on back plate to start it. Speedily, melody has developed to horsiness that be heard from gramophone's crackling needles. That perceive sound disrupts Jose, who is a local musician that has taken up his guitar, and perceives a sound of opening a rousing composition on strings or such like. He turns loud, and passionately strum the chords on a guitar as is drowning; but it's creaking the gramophone. Hearing the boom of a drum is flattering to those beat, in the rhythm of the South American dances, singing melody.

ANDRÉ
(Addresses Mathias.)
The man plays well up the strings of that takes your soul to fly! From what I seen he is a local? And yet, here's another talented musician!

MATHIAS
And you know how this, André? Have you been here, before?

ANDRÉ
(Is laughing.)
Like, you think I didn't! I have many years of sailing not like you're green? Mathias, get use to it?

Whilst the waitress, called Marisella who is in motion, at once delivered booze to those sailors.

André gave her tips; whilst Johnny takes a hand of this waitress, and asked her in a foreign dialect, in which Mathias is lost in translation.

ANDRÉ
What's your name, sweetheart?

MARISELLA
(Smiling coyly.)
Marisella! Seamen, you want to meet them?

ANDRÉ
(Turns his head to the girls.)
Yes! And the girlfriends of yours, what are they called?

MARISELLA
(Laughs.)
Veronica and Tijuana. What Sailor, do you like them to serve you're?

ANDRÉ
Not, really! But my friends are very captivated to get acquainted with them? What do you say to that?
(He turns to face the sailors, flickers.)

(PAUSE.)

Right, guys? Would you like to know the Mademoiselles' are named?

SAILORS IN CHORUS
Yes, we would it very much so, André! Ask, if she has other girlfriends...?

LIGHTS DIM.

————●◆※◆●————

After stage is well lit again all the decoration exact the same: actions in the bar "Flamingo". The lights fall into the place of bar's counter, where Marisol stood by.

From afar Mathias has notice a local girl, a young beauty with an olive skin - this is Marisol. She stood aside, is washing groceries and beer mugs.

Mathias became captivated, and is staring at her. He quickly rose of his sit, moves where she stood. Without thinking of daring he breaks the boundaries – he wants to talk to her. So, he is referring to this Bar's owner, and pokes his finger at the girl.

MATHIAS
Look, Boss, who is the girl that is standing over there?

At first Luis De Santos doesn't understands Mathias; then is realizing the essence, and he nods. He then is calling this girl in their local dialect.

LOUIS DE SANTOS
Hey, Amazonia, come on down, here?

Mathias finally spoke to this local young beauty. Though he does not understand they're local dialect. But it does not stop him; because he is eager than ever, get to know her, and to have her?

MATHIAS
I'm sorry, I do not understand your tongue? What is your name, beautiful?

This girl turns around; and looks to the other way.

MARISOL
Marisol! My name is Marisol!

MATHIAS
(He's excited.)
Look, Marisol, can I ask you to dance?

MARISOL
(Reluctantly, is talking with an accent.)
I'm sorry, señor, but I am working now, it's a policy, cause we workers now, it's a policy, cause we workers are not allowed to dance!

AWKWARD PAUSE.

MATHIAS
I'm sorry! I did not mean to hurt you, or for you to lose your job? Allow me take you home, after you end your shift, beauty? Do you agree, Marisol?

Mathias is enchanted by this girl's beauty. But he does not notice that she has exchanged glances with a young local, handsome man - Emanuel Amadeus.

He is seated there, aside, behind the counter. Emanuel is inherent muscular, and dressed in loose clothing that are accustomed to wear those inhabitants, in such like places and hot climates.

MARISOL
Fine, we will see after I finish working? In the meantime, I have to go back working!

MATHIAS
Thank you, beautiful! I'll wait for you?...

TRANSITION TO:

The stage well lit again. Once the show has ended, saw the sailors from the ship are on their way to leave.

Then and there André is referring to one of them.

ANDRÉ
Matt, what is it? Have you decided to stay here? Come with us man, let us all go back, to the ship?

MATHIAS
(Replies absently.)
No! No, you go guys ahead! I will catch up with you're later!

LIGHTS OUT.

SCENE 3.

On the stage change of attributes on scenery, where hard rebuild, and prepare to the next picture in a tent. It's view a Picture - night, the moon is shining. Personifying here a Tropical Edge.

In the far corner of the stage, added phenomenon of the Landscape: view of the Amazon River. Before the viewers' eyes appears a shack. Lights falls to where Mathias and Marisol are at the entry of her home.

MATHIAS

My beauty, kiss me! You put a spell on me? I've never be so attracted to any women, like I am to you?

MARISOL

(Turned away, talking to herself.)
What the foreigner is talking about? It would be better, if he gave me money?

MATHIAS

What are you saying? I've not go a twig of your dialect! But, do you like me?

MARISOL

Just call me, Amazonia!

LIGHTS DIM.

———◆━◆◆━◆———

LIGHTS UP ON:

NARRATOR

Without even realizing it, Mathias Surprisingly, and in one go, falls in love with a young woman, local beauty, Marisol, whom he has met, as she's on-stud being called – Amazonia!

SCENE 5.

Here, the light falls on the shack. At the entrance into the stand see Mathias, who holds in his hand Marisol, is looking into her eyes, he says solemnly.

MATHIAS

I came here, my beauty, because I want live in this shack near, where you'll be! Can I do that? After all, I hope your family would not oppose me?

LIGHTS OUT.

NARRATOR

It's passed approximately thirty days, from the time when Matt's deserted the ship. Now he lives in Marisol's hut, somewhere but in the Tropics of the Amazon.

LIGHTS UP ON:

NARRATOR

In the shack, where Matt settled, sometimes would appear Marisol relatives. The shack be located outskirts of a town, near the site where it's being paved the path that leading to the Rainforest. As on the other side be located a busy coast of the Atlantic Ocean, and near Marisol's home.

LIGHTS OUT.

LIGHTS UP ON:

NARRATOR

Forgetting his promise to return on the ship firstly. And most importantly to go back in Homeland, and to his family, Mathias gets into the world of making love, and infatuated with a young local beauty, in a stud - Amazonia.

In the opposite corner appears Mathias alongside Marisol.

MATHIAS

This merry dance is our sacred, I'm keeping you like a mist to my heart as a fairy. So, have wine with me, girl, and become mine! On the night of a full moon was Transparent with a bloom that is dip as the foam feels repent as it clip in the waves.

Our first dance, you made me amazed. A fun dance me Beckons be brave you may recon I'm adoring you? My sacred for me! Amazonia Will us be tailed forever? While Stars were read, Enhance, have Wine with me girl, and become mine!

MARISOL

Despite the mood it has Nowhere to turn from, except for food? Farewell, no more of Childhood? Let it come to wow our

MARISOL

dreams for at least, when at times of a mist? Then in respite we're going to miss?

MATHIAS

Dance with me, let's look each other in the eyes! No need for words, the main language is love that can tell you all without words, what its meet not to fall? Awake as your gaze is muting the fact my stare is fruiting and will be telling you about me be amazed by you my beauty!

LIGHTS OUT.

ACT THREE.

SCENE 1.

On the stage is a small extension in the form of a ship; in the background we can see fragments of the deck. There is the pyramid and the guns; a rope, as well flags from foreign countries.

Here emerges the chief Navigator, Johnny. It's scenery of the mast below-deck, in the upper corner the audience sees captain of the ship "Jeannette", François.

Near to him stood doctor Carlos, who is amused, as his shoulders have popped out of the ship's clutch.

On the other side of stage visible sailor, Felipe, who is whistling with delight to the tune? Here is the Navigator, following Johnny shown up and he stood on the deck. He then turns to face the viewers. Closed eyes a hand hanging over his forehead, hides from a sunray; and Johnny gazes into a distance of the Ocean.

In the center emerges young Felipe that mops the deck. In the upper left corner midshipman, Ferdinand, and Gerard - the Naval officer. Here is also seen the first assistant. Lighting directed at the picture of white clouds, but no warnings of a Storm at sea. The Sun is in the zenith.

Suddenly, the Navigator, Johnny interrupts this whistling Felipe, rotates, is referring to a Midshipman, Ferdinand with a strong criticism his tone indicates, when he looks closely; shoved a finger in his mouth, and puts it up in the air like he checks weather vane.

JOHNNY
From what I see, the wind is quite impetuous. The
clouds have amassed in the sky? How shocking I

may sound, Midshipman, but in my forecast it's going to be an awful storm at sea!

Ferdinand looks oddly at Johnny; and says in disbeliefs.

FERDINAND
Are you certain, Navigator?

JOHNNY
I think so! I am not mistaken, sir!

PAUSE. He turns to face Filipe, as tackles him.

JOHNNY
Cabin boy, go down and find the Naval officer, and his assistant, you've to tell the Captain about the situation that might occur?

CABIN BOY
Are you sure the Navigator? This can't be true? Look up in the sky It's blue? There are not clouds?

JOHNNY
Put aside talking, Cabin boy! Do you fancy going in troubles to a battalion?

CABIN BOY
No, sir! I'll report at once of your concern to the Captain's assistant...

The cabin boy runs up to the Naval Officer, Gérard. There is André, who's gesturing with his hands to the sailors.

Ferdinand, meanwhile, a first Assistant to the Navigator, mumbles; and they're at once approached Johnny, but talks only the Midshipman - Ferdinand.

NAVAL GERARD
Why did you called on us, mate?

FERDINAND
(Loud and clear.)
Sir, the Navigator and I've to inform you about a problem? Johnny report!

JOHNNY
(Picks up, and continual.)
Yes! You see, as I was watching the sky, and so I think that a killer storm at sea is approaching us!

NAVAL GERARD
So, what's the problem, Johnny?

JOHNNY
Shouldn't we inform the Captain? So that storm will not take us by a surprise?

NAVAL GERARD
(He rotates, to face Felipe.)
Now, Felipe, go down to Captain's cabin, and tell him: we have a storm coming up! Did you get it, Felipe?

CABIN BOY
Yes, senior, Naval officer!

JOHNNY
Then descend to Capitan's cabin, and be quick?

CABIN BOY
I am already on my way!

Felipe then walks off, leaves behind those on the scene.

LIGHTS OUT.

The stage well lit as it's filled with bottles on a table and three chairs. The ship's Captain, Francois dressed in naval form; close by is seen the ship's Doctor, Carlos. Here is Francois and Carlos seated down at a table; and began playing cards; they're instantly got into gambling of Bridge, or Poker games. Now appears Felipe, as has quickly stepped in. Then he turns to face the audience, and speaks up.

CABIN BOY

I'm sorry, señor Captain! And you too, Doctor! Allow me report of a problem?

CAPTAIN

Report sailor, what's the problem?

CABIN BOY

Captain, and you Doctor! Naval Officer and Navigator asked me report that, it can begin a violent storm at Sea, soon?

CAPTAIN

It's good to know before hand! Let the crew know of it! I'll soon climb to the deck. Is it clear, sailor?

CABIN BOY

Yes, sir! I'll warn them! Can I go?

PAUSE. The Captain nods, as a sign of his consent.

CAPTAIN

Yes, and thanks, Felipe! You may go!

A hand hung down over his temple, a sea cadet did it in honor; having turned round, he walked off.

—◆◆◆◆—

After a brief Blackout - scene Highlights: two Sailors on the deck, who are leading the conversation, one is Matt.

MATHIAS
(He's turned to face the man.)
The Navigator, how do you know, when a storm will be?

JOHNNY
Sailor, I've got many years to go Sailing! I'm aware practically of all treachery at Sea per Caprices!

PAUSE. He stops; turns to face Matt, and is asking him.

JOHNNY
Let's talk about you, Matt, people said that you were born on the Sea, or not?

MATHIAS
That's right, chief Navigator! The sea is my passion! I've always wanted to go Sailing, but it was not easy to do that, it's either one thing has interfered, or something else?

Matt stops short; produces a smile; and he prolongs.

MATHIAS
Only now, my dream came true!

JOHNNY

Listen, Matt, only at first glance, it seems the Sea dream adventure, but, no!...

He stops short; takes a breaths; and prolongs telling.

JOHNNY

At times, the sea is peaceful, and submissive; but, then comes a point, it can kill you. The waves can reach up to eight meters height, if watching, and it might on the bottom of the sea. (He stops; breathes deeply, and prolongs.)

(PAUSE.)

If thou shalt not hardy, and fear to prevent you to deal with Sea storms, before you realize it's the end of you! But, if you can withstand a situation of hardship, then you'll become a good sailor!

LIGHTS OUT.

SCENE 2.

On the stage a fast change of scenery, symbolizing sea-storm: grey clouds; sound of a gusty Wind howls; burst of lightning, and a lot of attributes. Here visibility of a Storm that forces a sail swinging.

The Climaxes in part one idem what occurs on upper deck, where are seen a couple of the Sailors, including Mathias who is working to defy against a strong wind.

MATHIAS

Senor Midshipman, the wind is too strong? I fear that I'll be thrown overboard?

CAPTAIN
(Confidently.)
No fear, Sailor! Grab the ropes, and hold on to it!

FELIPE
Matt, this is my first entry into the open Sea! I have never been in such difficult situation?

JOHNNY
Guys! Throw - shoot a breeze, it's better if you seize the ropes, and keep up to resist a force by uneven hour, guys? If not, you'll be thrown overboard! Then you rattle, when tattle yourself on the bottom of the sea?

SAILORS IN CHORUS
Yes, sir! We do exactly that! We keep the ropes tough!

Here appears the Captain; and appeals to the viewers.

CAPTAIN
(He is facing the sailors.)
How you're holding up, dudes? Are you keeping up, yes?

SAILORS IN CHORUS
We're trying, señor Captain, too hold on to these ropes!

CAPTAIN
Stay close one-to-another, if the waves arrive it will be easier to hold balance! Keep stretch the ropes

then pull it to yourself, and hold on strong! Times
two: go for it, guys!

———————

After a brief blackout - change of scenery on the stage, and
increasingly highlights the picture of the day there: the Sun is
shining.

Here appears Matt that is looking out to the viewers; his hang
up over-forehead, covering eyes from the light; and he is looking
meticulously into a distance, where Horizon - mergers with the
Ocean into a single space. Following a short silence, Mathias
turned over, is asking the Midshipman, Johnny.

MATHIAS
Thanks a lot, Chief Navigator!

PAUSE. Johnny is smiling; flickers with a wink, when he nods in
the "OK" sign.

LIGHTS FADE.

END OF PART 1.

PART THREE

SCENE 1.

Now Light falls into the Centre; where Felipe is mopping the mast of a ship. Hearing the Cabin boy is singing. On the back of the stage is visible the Naval officer, Ferdinand.

On the opposite side of stage arrival of the Assistant to the Navigator, André. Further makes appear the Navigator, Johnny, skimming passing by. Except now is heard the singing Cadet, Felipe on the mast there.

FELIPE
Through storm the waves have thrown us in the sea: to the right side or to the left, who knows if only we can see? While our figures hold the balance wide? Then we might get to norm life and there to be revived? After storm subside, and we might survive? Amaze its weird so we're to a Grit, and learn more to tie up the ropes? I guess coming home the Sailors feel warm when

FELIPE
Kiss the lips of those Pretty girls. And yet, what for these Sailors to to miss is not the feast, but it's the Sea! Fancy, when anew caprice is on it's way to praise? They have met the Sea o'er for them to see?

Johnny drew attention to the Hall; his Palm hangs over-forehead, shielding his eyes, as he stares intently into a distance.

Mathias, sudden interrupts Cadet Felipe's song, as he's immediately turned to the Captain; but he is bewildered.

MATHIAS
Señor, Captain, I can see the shores, at a close distance?

CAPTAIN
That's how it is, Sailor! Once we get closer to a port, where the Tropical edge is few miles from Amazon river? Then we'll see what we can do there?

(PAUSE.)

Now, Sailors, listen to my command: all aboard! Sailors, get up on the upper deck, and get ready to moor 'Jeannette' to the river Banks!

Johnny is drawn to him; he turns around to face Gérard.

JOHNNY
Yes, Captain!

CAPTAIN
(Loudly, clearly meets jerky.)
As for the Navigator We are only a dozen miles from the main port in the Amazon! Assemble the whole crew on deck! As we Getting ready to moor "Jeannette" to the River Banks? Get hold of the ropes?

THE NAVIGATOR
(Access it; and rotates to the sailors.)
Yes, sir! Sailors, listen to Captain's Command! All climb on the upper deck! Next all of you're to line up there?

SAILORS IN CHORUS
Yes, the Navigator! All as one to get up on the deck!

THE NAVIGATOR
Raise Sails! Give the ship full move!

SAILOR #2
Yes, to raise the sails! There we're progressing with a full speed!

SAILORS IN CHORUS
The ship is to get a full move!

LIGHTS OUT.

LIGHTS UP ON:

NARRATOR
In the distant, where Tropical edge, in South America, where ship "Jeannette" has docked in's Bay, near the Banks of Amazon River!

LIGHTS DIM:

NARRATOR
Shortly after the arrival of the ship "Jeannette" on shores a group of Sailors are stepping out, and Mathias is also together with them.

LIGHTS UP ON:

After a brief blackout, on stage change of scenery; which have highlighted: picture of the day - the Sun hovers. A Painting: personifying the Tropical Region of the Amazon.

In the upper corner of the scene, added scenery - the emergence of the landscape: a view of the Amazon Forest.

SCENE 2.

On the stage change of scenery, hard covers: is a picture of the day. The Sun in the sky soars. A painting is shown the Tropical Region of the Amazon. In the upper corner of the stage, added the scenery-the surfacing of the landscape: a view of the sea.

———●◆◆◆●———

The stage is well lit again, where a change of scenery for: these sailors appear here that are walking slowly in the City square.

The sailors walk through many places, then stepping far off outskirts of the city. Though they pass through.

———●◆◆◆●———

A change of scenery, on stage seen Mathias in the company with the Sailors; they walk are looking around; whenever visit places, or anything in their mind to go ahead for.

Suddenly those Sailors have stopped by the scene, whereas seen from afar the tavern; but the place have resembled more to a bar, and it's called 'Flamingo'.

SAILOR #1

Hey, you're guys! We have already detoured all the central place in this town! Learn about trail that is leading into the Rain Forest in the Amazon?

ANDRÉ

(He talks as if is boring.)
Yes, so what? We learned that it's the mouth of the Amazon River. We will be in favor to look for anew place? There's All-stars! What do you say to that, Dudes?

André nods his head on the bar, and is winking.

SAILORS IN CHORUS

That's a great idea, brother!

SAILOR #2

What about thou new sailor, is it not your name, Matt?

PAUSE. Mathias has nodded his head, as a sign of 'OK'.

ANDRÉ

Are you coming with us, or not? Or you afraid of your wife, mate?

MATHIAS

I am not afraid! Of course, I'll come with you! Because I have never been to such places?...

The Sailors with a stare at him, next to each other; and they're begun laughing. See they're walking boldly into the Tavern, titled "Flamingo" - in backstage.

SCENE 3.

In the back of the stage is the bar's counter, stand in front of her desk and chairs, where, sit down those sailors. A bit far piece in the form of an Office of the restaurant; furnished with bottles at the table playing cards, regular customers or those locals.

Over the counter hanging the name of the bar: 'Flamingo'. The landlord of the bar, Louise de Santos, abruptly walks around, to be ensured there is order in. Here, the host bar is the place, where stands an old gramophone; he puts on the back plate, and starts it.

Immediately it's become hoarse sound of music be heard from the crackling needles, while reaching a melody is not entirely clear.

Curtly, the horsiness of melody be heard from gramophone interrupts by Jose is a local musician, who's taken up his guitar, and perceives a sound of starting like a rousing music up on his strings. Jose turns louder as has passionately strummed on a guitar's chords, is drowning; and creaking that gramophone.

Hearing the boom of drum is flattering to those beat, in

the rhythm of the South American dances, singing melody.

ANDRÉ
(Addresses Mathias.)
The man plays well up the strings of that takes your soul to fly! From what I can see he is a local? And yet, he is another talented musician!

MATHIAS
And you know how, André? Have you been here already?

ANDRÉ
Like I have not! What you think? I've got many years
of sailing, not like you're green? Mathias, get use to it?

Jose just stopped playing the guitar, and the waitress immediately
Marisella be in motion, delivered booze to those sailors.

Meantime, André is given some tips; and Johnny takes the
waitress's hand, has asked her in a foreign language. In this idiom
Matt here has being lost in translation.

ANDRÉ
What's your name, sweetheart?

MARISELLA
(Smiling coyly.)
Marisella! What, do you want to meet, Seamen?

ANDRÉ
(Turns his head towards the girls.)
Yes! As the girlfriends of yours, what are they
called? André

MARISELLA
(Laughs.)
Veronica and Tijuana. What is it sailor, do you
want them to serve you're?

ANDRÉ
Not really! But my friends will be interested to get
familiar with them? Well, what do you say, guys?

PAUSE. He then turns to face those sailors, and gave a wink.

Am I spot-on, sailors? Would you like
to know those girls names?

SAILORS IN CHORUS
Yes, we would very much so, André! Ask, if she has
other girlfriends...?

LIGHTS DIM.

After it's well lit again all the decoration exact the same: here
scenery: Events in a bar "Flamingo". Here lights fall onto a place
in the bar, whereas Marisol stood at the end corner of that counter.

From afar Mathias has notice a local girl, a young beauty with olive
skin - this is Marisol. She stood aside, is washing groceries and beer
mugs.

Amazingly Matt became captivated, and is staring at her. He
quickly rose of his sit, and moves to where she stood. Without
thinking of be bold, Matt breaks the boundaries - he wants to meet
her, and yet refers to the Bar's owner.

MATHIAS
(Referring pokes his finger at her.)
Look, Boss, who is the girl that stands over there?

At first Luis De Santos doesn't understands Mathias. When he
is realizing the essence, and he nods his head. He at once starts
calling this girl on their local dialect.

LOUIS DE SANTOS
Hey, Amazonia, come on, here?

Mathias finally spoke to this local young beauty. Though doesn't
stop him, he is eager than ever get to know her.

MATHIAS
I'm sorry, I do not understand your language?
What's your name, beauty?

Now, she turns around, and looks to the other way.

MARISOL
Marisol! My name is Marisol!

MATHIAS
(Is excited.)
Look, Marisol, can I ask you to dance?

MARISOL
(Reluctantly, is talking with an accent.)
I'm sorry, señor, but I'm working now, it's policy
for workers we're not allowed to dance with clients?

MATHIAS
I'm sorry! I did not mean to hurt you, or for you
to loose your job? Let me take you home, after you
end your shift? Do you agree, beautiful?

Mathias is enchanted by girl's beauty; but he does not notice that
she has exchanged glances with a young local, handsome man -
Emanuel Amadeus. He sits, but on the sidelines, behind counter.
Emanuel is dressed in loose clothing, and inherent, which are used
to wearing those inhabitants, in such like places and hot climates.

MARISOL
Okay, we will meet after work? In the meantime, I
have to go back to work!

MATHIAS
Yes! Thank you, beautiful! I'll wait on you?…

LIGHTS DIM.

The stage is well lit again. When the show ended, have seen the sailors from 'Jeannette' on their way to leave. There is one of Matt's friends, André, and refers to him.

ANDRÉ
Matt, what is it? Are you intend to stay? Come man! Let's go with us?

MATHIAS
(Reacts absently.)
No, you go guys ahead! I will catch with you later!

SCENE 4.

On the stage change of attributes on scenery where hard rebuild, and prepare a scene to anew picture in a tent. Here view is the Night in Paradise full moon over shiny.

Personifying here in the far corner of the stage, added phenomenon image of the landscape it's the Tropical Edge, where view of the Amazon area in the Rainforest.

Before viewers' eyes develops a shed. It's well lit falls to where Mathias and Marisol at the entrance of her home.

MATHIAS
My beauty, kiss me, you have put a spell on me? I never been so attracted to any women, like I am to you?

MARISOL
(Turned away, talking to herself.)
What the stranger keeps talking? It'd be better, if he gave me money?

MATHIAS
What are you saying? I do not know your dialect!
But, do you like me?

MARISOL
Just call me, Amazonia!

LIGHTS DIM.

————◆◆◆◆◆————

LIGHTS UP ON:

NARRATOR
Without even realizing it, Mathias unpredictably,
in one go, he falls in love with a young, local
beauty - Marisol that, on-stud, Amazonia.

LIGHTS FADE.

SCENE 5.

Saw on the mast; and a small outbuilding in the form of ship that,
also serves as the upper deck.

Here, comes to the attention ship's captain and Ferdinand– the
Midshipman. On the background saw the sailor André, there's still
is the Navigator, Johnny.

At this time in front of viewers appears a local man with a pierced
left ear, Diego. He is introduced himself as the messenger; however,
he's talked with an accent.

DIEGO

Señor sailors, sorry, can allow me to climb up on your ship?

Hearing the ship's Captain refers to Diego from the deck.

CAPTAIN

What's your excuse to coming up here? And who are you?

DIEGO

Señor, sailors! I'm Diego, and the messenger that brought you a letter from one of your mates?

The Captain goes down the stairs, from the upper corner. Now he appears on the deck.

Diego stretches his hand, gives a paper is folded square, in Gerard's hand. Diego stretches his hand with a paper is folded square, and into Gerard's hand. Then Gerard has struck up to say, but he's been stopped by the Captain's commanding voice.

CAPTAIN

Gerard, wait! Listen, man, your name is Diego?

PAUSE. Diego nods his head, as a sign of consent.

CAPTAIN

What else he told give our sailor? Did he ask you to convey in words to us?

BEAT. Now Diego pullouts from his pocket a letter.

DIEGO

No, Señor! Matt gave me a letter, and said to pass the message that he has decided to stay!

PAUSE. Diego gives a note to François; and he prolongs.

DIEGO

Matt only asked me to tell you not to look for him, as you won't find him! The ship is set to be sailing without him! Now I've to run, a job awaits! Jolly, and happy tailwind for us!

LIGHTS DIM.

———◆✦⋈✦◆———

Lights well lit. Once this local, Diego has left on the deck-begun debates amid those Sailors and manning are of the control of this ship "Jeannette".

CAPTAIN

What did happen Midshipman? You've walked close to sailor, Marceau? What can you tell us about, the Navigator? And you too, the Midshipman?

FERDINAND

Captain, we went for a walk together in the city. After, all of us went to a bar 'Flamingo', where we drank beer.

PAUSE. He is with a stare, it seems if he is recalling something.

FERDINAND

If I'm not wrong that place was called 'Flamingo'? Yes! Sailors, back me up?

The Sailors nod, as a sign. Now Johnny has a word to say.

JOHNNY

Captain, and you gentlemen, when we were in the pub, there unobtrusive nothing seems be wrong? Mathias was sitting with us, but drank a little.
(He stops; takes a deep breath; and prolongs.)
(PAUSE.)

JOHNNY

When time was for us leaving, I asked Matt to come with us, but he refused and said: that was not going with the crew, as he'll catch up with us later?

Suddenly, André intervenes, and is revealing a secret about Mathias to one and all there.

ANDRÉ

Captain, I have a word to say?

Francois is nodded. And André begins to tell his story.

ANDRÉ

I recall now, Matt has noticed a girl, a local beauty there. He's even spoke with her! Well, he is a man and so am I! I'm aware that he was away for a while, maybe desperate, and in need to have Sex? Who knows, what they're cooking? I didn't try to nurse him?

PAUSE. Then it seems that something has struck to him.

ANDRÉ

Maybe it's the reason, why he wants to remain here, just to be with her? What about his wife and children? What we shall tell them, about it?

CAPTAIN

Wait! Do not jump to a conclusion! Let me read his letter? Then we'll find out exactly, what's gone wrong?

Francois's face turn serious, he bows his head, and is reading from the note aloud.

CAPTAIN

"Captain! I quit the ship, and would not return home. Tell my wife and the children to forgive me for everything? Goodbye, and thank you! Mathias." Be followed by his signature.

PAUSE. After all looked at each other at a complete loss.

LIGHTS FADE.

SCENE 6.

Here, the light falls on the shack. At the entrance into the stand see Mathias, who holds in his hand Marisol's hand; and is looking into her eyes.

MATHIAS
(Talks solemnly.)

I came here, my beauty, because I want to live in a shack near where you will be! Can I do that? After all, your relatives would not oppose me?

LIGHTS DIM.

———◆◆◆◆———

NARRATOR

It pass around 30 days, from the moment that Matt jumped the ship. Now he lives in Marisol's shed, somewhere in the tropics and near the Atlantic ocean...

LIGHTS DIM.

LIGHTS UP ON:

NARRATOR

In a hut, where Mathias's settled, sometimes would appear Marisol's relatives. The shack was outskirts of town, near the site, where be paved the path, that is leading to the Amazon Rainforest. While on other side, it's be located on a busy coast of the Atlantic Ocean and near, where Marisol's home was.

LIGHTS DIM.

LIGHT UP ON:

NARRATOR

Forgetting his promise to return on the ship first, but importantly back in his homeland, and to his family –Mathias gets into the world of making making love, enjoying it with a young, local beauty, in stud - Amazonia.

In the opposite corner - appear Matt alongside Marisol.

MATHIAS

The merry dance is sacred, I'm saving it for last. Do you fancy me? Whilst my heart fills with you, as a fairy! So, have Wine with me, Girl, and become mine! On the night of a full moon - the Luna Transparent with Bloom, just as the foam is might flip to make waves. Our first dance, you gave me amaze.

MATHIAS

Fun dances as me beckon to be brave as making love to you? My sacred recon that I share with you! Amaze as the Stars were read. So, we were you? Have more fine Wine with me, girl - and become mine!

MARISOL

Despite of the mood it has nowhere to go - a Farewell to Childhood? Let it come in our dreams at least sometimes! At times as its a mist, but later in respite, we are going to miss?

Matt scratched his head, as if is thinking. He states.

MATHIAS

What is wrong with me? Am I in love? No! It cannot be? What about my wife and the kids that are waiting for me in my homeland?

MARISOL

(Twists; whispers to herself.)
Why stranger moved in? He would be better given me the money!

MATHIAS

What are you saying? I do not understand your tongue? But, do you like me, Marisol, right?

———◆◈◆———

MATHIAS

Dance with me, let's look Each other in the eyes! No need for words, main language is my love, which can tell you all without words what mead not to fall? Awake as your gaze is muting. The fact my stare will tell - of me be bewitched by you, my beauty!

———◆◈◆———

MARISOL

(In Spanish to herself.)
What the foreigner is talking about? But he still would not give me the money?

LIGHTS OUT.

SCENE 7.

On stage change of scenery, where the chaise parked; here Well lit. Inside appears a young couple is passionately in conversation. Where saw Marisol; next to her sits a young handsome, local man, his name - Emanuel Amadeus.

EMANUEL

I hate that visitor drags everywhere after you? We can't even see each other, as often as before, Marisol?

MARISOL

My love, tomorrow we'll take on the Carnival. We'll meet there, and decide how to proceed with it? What do you think about that? Do you agree? Say yes, Emanuel?

EMANUEL

Okay, put up one more day. But from tomorrow on, I don't want you to see the foreigner any more. Do you fathom, Amazonia? Let him send, whence he has sailed to us from?

MARISOL

Yes, my dearest! Then, let's not waste time? Love me passionately, dear!

EMANUEL

Yes! Let's make love all night...

Following, as they're begun kissing passionately...

LIGHTS DIM.

SCENE 8.

NARRATOR

It's the Seacoast not far from Marisol's hut, where Mathias has also resided...

There's change of scene as is rebuilt in the Main Square of the parade, where is the emergence of those natives.

* The sounds of music appears with leisurely crowd, is dressed in colorful national folklore inherent to the places; lights is around

sparking. Overall multicolored scenery juggles, fakirs with metal torches of fire, as they're releasing fire out-of-mouth.

Here appears Mathias that walks alongside Marisol.

MATHIAS

Dance with me! Let's look each other in the eyes! No need for words, the main semantic is for us - to be Romantic? Love tells you all without words, what mead not need for me to fall? You awake of my gaze it is muting? In fact my stare will tell you all, me mere amazed by you, my beauty! Amazonia, you're great kisser that's, I'm a slither? Cause you're driving me to be hissing! Oh, you're my daisy!

There appears another crowd, is moving slowly, through. As the pair at the same time continue to dance, and a twist their bodies. There seen Diego, the messenger, with an earring, he observes, movements of the crowd keenly; like it - are equally hilarious.

It can be seen at distance in the crowd, where a young, handsome local man – Emanuel moves; he winks to Marisol; Markedly. She gradually became distanced from Mathias. And all of sudden, she's disappeared from the view. Stage well lit.

Mathias remains individually as it pushes into the crowd, which is lively and fun, when they ran past him. He rotates; is looking for someone, be drunk.

MATHIAS

Marisol, where are you?

The Stage Well-lit again, where's a change of scenery. There is a hut sited is on the side, near the town, which hosted the New build path to the forests, in the Amazon.

Mathias enters the hut where he Marisol live together... But Marisol has not yet appeared there. Mathias be in disbelief, and said to himself.

MATHIAS
Marisol, has not yet appeared here? Have we lost each other on the parade?

BLACKOUT.

After a brief blackout the stage well lit, where is seen Mathias sits down on the floor? All those times he was waiting in their gazebo, for Marisol to arrive.

NARRATOR
It has past long time, but Amazonia still did not appear. AS Mathias is kept glancing at his watch.

Here begins the sound of a sad melody.

LIGHTS DIM.

SCENE 9.

On stage change of scenery, where the chaise parked; here Well lit; inside appears a young couple is passionately in a conversation. There saw Marisol. Next to her sits a young handsome local man, his name - Emanuel Amadeus.

MARISOL
(Speaks in Spanish.)
Don't worry, my love! I do not want him. I only lured him for money. Have a bit of patience, as he'll be going back on his ship, soon? Then, we will have money to meet our dreams?

EMANUEL
I hate that the outsider drags everywhere after you? We can't even see each other, as often as before?

MARISOL
My love, tomorrow we'll come to the Carnival. You and I'll meet there, and decide how to proceed with it? What do you think about that? Do you agree? Say yes, Emanuel?

EMANUEL
Okay, put up one more day. But from tomorrow on, I don't want you to see the foreigner any more. Do you fathom, Amazonia? Let him send, whence he has sailed to us from?

MARISOL
Yes, my dearest! Then, let's not waste time? Love me passionately, dearest!

EMANUEL
Yes! We'll love each other all night!

LIGHTS DIM.

There is a change of scenery. On Stage resumes a picture the night full of stars. Saw moonlight is reflecting, and flashing down, into the clear waters of the Sea.

Seacoast not far from Marisol's home, where Mathias has also resided.

Here lights fall on Mathias, who still sits on the floor; he's head bowed down, is tensely held head in his hands, constantly shakes up and down, and talks to himself.

MATHIAS

Why Marisol, does not come? What could happen with her?

Then rising up from the floor, Mathias quickly goes out.

LIGHTS OUT.

ACT III

SCENE 1.

The Stage is redecorated: change of scenery a picture: fragments of a ship's deck. In this act those sailors, are; still there observable the Naval officer wearing uniform. The stage Well-lit: action is taken place on ship's deck; whereas appears captain Francois.

On the opposite site, are the Navigator - Johnny and his assistant, André rushing.

CAPTAIN
Well, gentlemen, we have not found our sailor Marceau? Because of him, crew lingered in Tropics more than we've planned. Seamen, it's time for us to cast off from this region. Now, lift, the anchor! As we sailing off!

JOHNNY
Yes, sir, to lift the anchor!

CAPTAIN
Giving, mooring! A full forward!

ANDRÉ
There is full go, and sailing off!

SAILOR #2
Yes, in a full speed to sail off!

SAILORS IN CHORUS
Yes, in a full, go ahead, sailing off!
(Be heard echoes.)
In a full speed, sailing off!

LIGHTS OUT.

On Stage lights fall on Mathias, wandering through the rainforest. Picture appears, where Mathias walks on the stage, looking, he carefully examines all around, as if looking for someone. Then, Mathias goes backstage. Changing scenery, on the stage - the picture of a town appears in the foreground of Mathias, is wandering alone, pacing the stage. He is shouting, and calling for her.

MATHIAS
Amazonia, where are you? Let me hear your voice,
lovely, Marisol! Amazonia, where are you? Let me
hear your voice, lovely, Marisol!

———◆◆◆◆———

LIGHTS UP ON:

After a brief blackout it is a picture: Morning, sun up. Here lights fall on Mathias, is wandering near seashore. He looks tired, depressed, and says impatiently

MATHIAS
Where Marisol can be? I have searched practically
all the places that were familiar? But, I'm not a
local. I'll try to inspect all the places? But I have
never walked to, so far?

As a beast of prey, lying in wait for target, Matt creeps silently, to the dwelling; sometimes crouching to him, it seems is unnoticed within the bushes. Approached a sudden, where before Mathias eyes is emerged a picture, affecting his imagination.

PAUSE. Quickly is crouching, Matt hides in the bushes.

MATHIAS
(Whispering to him.)
Oh, my God! This cannot be? Or I could be
imagining things? It can't be true? But it is
Amazonia, there?

He moves in his sit. And he takes a position to watch.

MATHIAS
I'll sit and wait here? This way I can overhear them?
Though, I do not understand a damn thing, what
they are saying in their language?

LIGHTS OUT.

SCENE 2.

Here a quick change of scenery, the stage is set: inside the shed.
The Stage lights Marisol appeared there, and is sitting next to a
local, young Emanuel. Marisol, warm hugs and kisses with young,
handsome - Emanuel.

The Scene Clarifies Mathias contrary, in the bush at this time,
rising up, he went slowly and silently, is a hovel.

Still, Emanuel peeks Matt's presence, first.

Here, Marisol is sitting beside him, but with her back to the
entrance. Emanuel, however, is staring at Mathias with a shrewdly
smirk. Emanuel turns, and tackles her.

EMANUEL
(Is kissing her; speaks in Spanish.)
Marisol, who owns your heart? Go now, say
exactly, who do you love?

MARISOL

Honey! My heart belongs to you! I belong only to one, you Emanuel!

At this point, Mathias mad, blinded by jealousy, he grabs Marisol's hand and throws it on the ground; is addressing her angry tone, but he looks pale; says angrily and loud

MATHIAS

What are you doing here? I have not slept all night, was worried, Marisol, and looked for you? But you having fun with this fool? Oh, you a whore!

MARISOL

Nobody asked you, foreigner, to come in here! I'm a free woman, and do what I like! I can have fun too, with whom I want too! Do you understand?

EMANUEL

(Speaks in Spanish.)
Amazonia, why did he insult you? What does he want? Ask him to leave at once?

MARISOL

He's said that was looking for me all night! I told him I'm a free woman, do what I want, and love who I want!

EMANUEL

Tell the stranger it's our native language! We're all here speak our language! Delivery (communicates) he is ignorant to our dialect?

PAUSE. He looks be anger at Matt; and prolonged.

EMANUEL

If he does not understand our tongue, let him go back to where has sailed off! Nobody here has invited him?

MATHIAS

Marisol, why are you talking in strange tongue? I do not understand you're?

MARISOL

Peregrine, you do not understand our Native language? It's too bad! In that case why don't you go to from where you have sailed!

PAUSE.

MATHIAS

This bastard has said straight that? Oh, he is a scoundrel!

MARISOL

Yes! And I think the same! Stranger, go back to the ship, and swim back to your homeland!

BLACKOUT.

———◆◆◇◆◆———

LIGHTS UP ON:

Here lights fall on Mathias, his head began to spin; he is imagining bud be again in the sea; where began pitching, and him caught in a heavy storm.

Mathias puts a hand deep into his pocket, and felt there a pistol. He then pulls out a gun. Enhanced the lights to she is seen a weapon in the hands of Mathias.

Marisol and her young lover are scared now, when she shouts to stop him; but he is like deaf ear to her plea.

MARISOL
Mathias, why do you hold a weapon? What are you going to do with it?

Aiming Matt shoots emphasis on Emanuel; he directly began sinking slowly. Falling Emanuel is frozen in a dead pose.

On the spot, Marisol is shaken Emanuel's dead body.

MARISOL
(Is shaken the dead boy.)
Oh, you bastard! What have you done? Why you killed him?

PAUSE. She stops; is crying, points a hand at Emanuel.

MARISOL
Emanuel is my only love! Damn you, outsider! Curse you three times!

LIGHTS DIM.

After a brief DIM the Stage Well Lit, Mathias is slowly come to life? Now he has realized the words that Marisol said - it's shocked, and painfully wounded his heart.

MATHIAS
What did you say? But how can I, Amazonia? What should I do with my feeling for you, pray tell?

Marisol does not look at him; it's little effort in the face of her dead.

MARISOL
You a murderer! I never loved you!

PAUSE. She then bows down; and attend to a dead man.

MARISOL
Emanuel, my love, open your eyes! What would I do, without you?

She is crying, and shaken a dead boy on the ground. Matt is with a plea looks; he's hands crossed up on his chest.

MATHIAS
Amazonia, I love you! I didn't love so anyone, as I do you? I deserted my ship! Threw out in homeland my family! As to get you fall in love me?

MARISOL
How I despise you, for what you did? Damn you! Outsider, get out of here!

MATHIAS
If so, you refuse my love Amazonia? Then die together with your lover!

Mathias taking aims and shoots Marisol. Seen she's slowly lowered down, but moves closer to Emanuel's body. Marisol immediately dies next to her lover.

At the same time, as she has stroked this young man's face, while her hand does freeze on the spot - in the dead pose.

Matt has pictured, as if he was going mad. An assumption of what he has committed by killing; Mathias falls down to his knees before Marisol, is sobbing from agony of broken hearted.

LIGHTS FADE.

SCENE 4.

The stage changes to anew scenery: In the Bar. The Scene Well lit; it's mounting a couple of tables with stools.

In the back of the stage, scene: In the bar, there are installed rack; tables and chairs, where sits Mathias. On top over the counter with inscription - 'Flamingo'.

Here's Universal Fun. Wine drinking. Jose is holding the guitar and plays, as sits on stool behind the counter.

Only Matt still is motionless with a wine glass that held in his hand; as he looks through the glass of the tank. Mathias's fixed his gaze upwards to the light.

MATHIAS
What have I done? I killed her! Oh, Marisol, forgive me! Am I in Hell…?

Mathias has imagined, as he was going mad. Taken in that he committed a murder. So he drops to his knees in front of Marisol, is sobbing, and groaning loud from suffering.

———— •◆×◆● ————

After a delay stage Well Lit – sees Mathias in fantasies.

MATHIAS
What I have heard then acted on it! But be haunted
me? It's a nightmare? When I wake up, the whole
thing will hark back as it was afore?

LIGHTS OUT.

After a brief blackout - the Stage well lit - it's rack, where sits
Mathias in "Flamingo". Now the lights fall to where suddenly
appear Sofia, who stood in a bar, where by Matt's sit on counter.
Sofia is a mysterious emergence?

MATHIAS
That stormy till goes to the left, then lays to the
right. Sailfish on waves might be an endless guide.
He was selected by the Sea. Everlasting, but zealous -
if we can only see?

SOFIA
And for, we can see how Sand of time slips down
the hourglass. With the mind full has missed more
hourglass be cruel with time? It has feast then pass
thru mass moments. For it goes down: most there
no win situation? Nethermost as it's force to see the
day light? We might predict the fate of one! But
fight to escape or to corrupt is nobody can forsake?

MATHIAS
(He is amazed.)
Gypsy lady, how did you get here? Can all this be a
nightmare, and you have been haunting me?

SOFIA

Yes and no, Mathias! You're partly Daydreaming?
As I am here for real, and stand before you!

PAUSE. Sofia stops short; looks at Mathias with pity, she then prolongs with her story.

SOFIA

Sailor, I told you once that I could predict future
and fate of the people, unless there's not?

MATHIAS

Yes! Why did you come? What else do you want
from me, Lady? Is it not enough to see that I am
in pain? Back then, in vein, you were right in-all,
at the Fair, you warned me! And now I became a
killer?

SOFIA

No, sailor! But, on one thing you right. Then
and there you did not listen e? Laughed at my
Prophecy? You have not behaved rational and in a
jealous rage with this girl?

MATHIAS

I know, I know as I'm going crazy! My soul spot in
mud - I fought, but lost, daisy is not mine. For I've
to Flout, but Neglect and forget, how I behaved?
Now, Lady, you understand?

LIGHTS DIM.

———◆►✕◄◆———

LIGHTS UP ON:

Matt puts his hands forward as a bud - he wants to pray.

SOFIA
Yes! Listen to me at least now?

———◆›◆‹◆———

SOFIA
Oh, if only twice we would Enter the same
Riverbank? Only life experience could Bring
under-hour epiphany! As a spank is symphony! I
feel to be under the wings at times, when we'd be
true to ourselves? Then I can be healed.

For years it's pushing us toward the river so as to
cross it knowing live. Whiled in the way wiser as
fight for more, but not to get milled. As a reward of
credo for Being wise, we might have fall deep into
crisis!

PAUSE.

MATHIAS
It frightens me, toward The end of my existent, The
woman's eyes that Is in love with me, it's Isabel'!
But most of all my children hurtful words? Though
they're faraway that made of flesh and blood?

SOFIA
It's worse, why not to ask your conscience about?
Were you afraid? That your Remorse could fade
away? Unless there's a thunder Spectacle but the
anxiety

SOFIA

Make you strong? I wonder if I'm wicked? Or it's felt that you've been tricked?

MATHIAS

Dear Gypsy lady, you're as Always right, because I'm Nomad! And all my vows have been now downright for Maud! Words of regret might be Empty! The only way is to Forget is sacrifice myself, but will reverse felt real? As only act to rationalize myself if it could be modified? In what mood would it pass? Plus the Mass will save us all from fuss?

<hr />

MATHIAS

Can all this be a nightmare that haunted me, around?

SOFIA

No! You were partly daydreaming? Mathias, I am here for real, and I stand in front of you!

PAUSE. She stops short; looks with pity. Now he parleys.

MATHIAS

You were right in all, back then At fair, when you have warned me, It's nightmare now? What just ensued. Did you anticipated, lady?

SOFIA
(Shakes her head.)

No, Mathias!

MATHIAS

When I wake up I'll be in jail, right?

SOFIA

On one thing you right, and the only advice I can
give you, is not to get more drunk?

———◆◆◆◆◆———

SOFIA

Matt! Oh, Matt! Go back to your family! And the
Sea will Bless in a way? When your arrival on the
go that no one can see! But, don't forget on your
way home the swing went a thousand times ahead.
Mayhap is folding in the Arc - like it's long had its
way into the dark. Anyway, Mathias, you too by
power, have gone to smudge a few!

PAUSE. Sofia stops; it seems that she feels for him.

SOFIA

So, you have figured out, sailor From the fate no-
one, no-one, Can ever escape!

———◆◆◆◆◆———

After a brief Blackout - the stage Well-lit; and lights fall to where
suddenly appears Marisol. She is dressing in blue lightly clothing;
following her is Mathias.

NARRATOR

In a faraway land, where the Amazon is located,
it's Natives created a Tale Vis-a-vis on love? How
a grey-eyed foreign man, who's sailed for miles
the Sea - fall for a girl be so-called Amazonian
beauty! Whiles we will not miss them to see! As
it felt tale be immoral, But it has not failed, and
best remained enduring? Since time has no power
Over-telling?

NARRATOR
Never mind if name of this story is over-telling?
Never mind, if name of this story is the unrequited
Love!

LIGHTS FADE.

———◆▸◂◆———

END OF PART 2.

PART FOUR

<u>SCENE 1.</u>

It views the officers are wearing their uniforms. Stage Well-lit: at the moment on the ship appears Francois; where, on the opposite side stood the Navigator - Johnny, and his assistant, André'; on one side is another sailor.

Next appears Gerard, when makes a turn to face audience; that squints, is Palm-sized, hanging over his forehead; and covers the eyes, peering into the distance, where the Horizon merges with the Ocean - in a single space.

NARRATOR
Near Port in Brazil with fine pine and coffee grain
on-board - 'Jeannette' was slowly mooring to the
Fort.

Just as the ship came in the Port, debarked - that
fine Sea crew has embarked on shores. And there
be greeted! Going slouch, when they've marched in
a street parade!

Better than sitting in hand with bog on a couch.
And so they went to meet those narrow skirts!
Ouch, who are cracking fata, but crew that May
miss the strata?

LIGHTS DIM.

LIGHTS UP ON:

NARRATOR

Yet, few Seamen went, too where anyone mere with
no cant will be easily hooked up with womenfolk
and fine wine. Where beers foam, and drinks
pomp, they do fall for those in narrow skirts, as
they're cracking into their Joints!

LIGHTS DIM.

SCENE 2.

Meanwhile, in the shared saloon the owner Tijuana is teaching her
girls how to welcoming men clients – inn.

TIJUANA

Making Love is basis of Life! What's the point to
deny as you facing? You're taken it, and be seduced
by that's aim for. Let's be bold and strip it naked?
Don't refuse to be seduced. You dare up to fly like a
rocket in the sky through

Mid-night and grip. As be given yourself without
Love is mere faking. In a Love is making? Then in
a blink of an eye a heart pump as it's not faking?

Bah, it's not fair for them to think you'd make it?
On a whim - you and Him… Trembling lips.
Rambling – then slowly into drift. In the heat of
the night, when meet, then it creeps.

TIJUANA

Entrance into the zone, and breaks. Makes for Inland, but fakes. Moan as its tore into hemisphere! Rigging more. And we're digging with the aim - for gold!

Sliding on-waves, tilting when painting, but rigging against storms at Sea! Why not come visit "Tijuana"? I reckon you can become free! Beckon, as you'll feel in here a sensation!

WOMAN #1

Caressing fingers. Feels Hot breathe. Palm-to-hip Ratio. Whilst Dollars Currencies in a valise feels your spirits is deep! Release and bon voyage!

TIJUANA

How, do you do? Girls, what's your respond should sound, Veronica?

WOMAN #1

Making love is basis of being! Oh, yes! Sir, for you I can do!

DRAG QUEEN

We'll make your desires come true! As my wish to come in too? I'll do it for you!

TIJUANA

Men and I are mirage! Girls are you ready for my important guests?

WOMEN IN CHORUS

Yes, mistress! We're ready to battle!

A severe style owner of the Tavern/Night Club, Tijuana's travel is combined with striptease by those workwomen.

Now is seen the reaction of those male customers to that spectacle, which eyes are bulging, and mouths open.

Nearby view the young women that are wearing brief skirts; but they having acted in pretty immodest way to those clienteles.

SAILOR #1
That stormy till to the left, then it puts to the right!

SAILOR #2
Sailfish on waves might be a vast guide. He was fast and Zealous chosen by Sea, endless ban, as only fellows may see?

———◆━×━◆———

Sudden André from the French sailors peeks in the window somewhat, began shouting.

ANDRÉ
Stop it! Everybody scram! All of you're, and I mean it!

Then the English sailor, Ben runs to the window, and began waving his hands up in the air.

GORDON
He is right! Sailors, stop the Combat at once, all of you are!

CHARLES
I'm completely gutted with that situation? It's nothing for me inhere?
(He then turns round to find Englishmen.)

(PAUSE.)

CHARLES
Sailors, let's go back to our ship, or else? Let us swim to discover the new India? (BEAT.)

SAILOR #3
Everybody, let's get the Hell out Of this gory Club! All of you're?

The reporter has not even finished as the Policeman interrupts his gestures, as is mimicking to De Costa. The Policeman named, De De Costa holds a finger to his lips, talks in a half-whisper.

POLICEMAN
Shush-Shush!

LIGHTS OUT.

———◆►⊯◄●———

LIGHTS UP ON:

Meanwhile, at interior of a tavern, Veronica opens up.

DRAG QUEEN
In my dreams it's no longer epic exist, only a lonely Midshipman was kissed? Whilst in the heart of a wanderer - coolness, it seals with ice floes – but with fullness of blows?

The way to my home has gone and forgotten! Yet I'm unloved. There's no return be acted It's fiction, not remorse! The core to a solution Jurisdiction? For me chose Profession as my relations say a disgrace! Mean as my family is dubious for me to quit! Maze me be in trance!

WOMAN #3
Thus made me be in despair, if worlds forsake true love? Fold in been solo, or you follow others to Mars? Bold as the myths vaporize into the hollow!

ANDRÉ
It was a majestic mirage, but my soul feels forlorn? You can hear that the Sea rinse up, as we paddle on. Whilst me alone a wanderer with the skills be money Launderer it seems I'm an adrift shuttle in a feud? Then, why do I stay in this God forsaken place that have made me into a slewed?

FERDINAND
So, do not go there, where you'll get hold of women and fine wine. There beer foam, and drinks pomp it doesnot feel those narrow skirts are cracking by it's joint!

SAILORS IN CHORUS
It's a farce, as us to go behind bars? No, way! So, do not go there, where you can easily get hold of your draw more to women and fine wine...

LIGHTS FADE.

SCENE 3.

When the scene is illuminated: a little off-piece cabinet in saloon, where at the table, laden with dishes, playing poker or Bridge: Naval Officer Gerard. Ferdinand; near is a local, and cadet, Felipe. Over the counter hangs a name 'Tijuana'.

Innkeeper appears is not a young woman, and keeps on PRAM a cigarette and smoking, she is the owner of the establishment

"Tijuana", as she crawls around tensely. She is saluting with Champagne on the fly glasses to those patrons and regular men, who are sipping alcohol. Sound in the rhythm of the Jazz of Latin American melody. The waitresses are carrying drinks, or stood washing glasses and mugs, aside. There are few young women in short skirts, and they behave pretty uninhibited to those clienteles.

Now "Tijuana" is entering seven English sailors. Once finding places, they are seated on other side of the bar's counter.

LIGHTS OUT.

———◆◆◆◆◆———

Meanwhile, outside comes into view a group of local Governed, one among them is the Governor. All are afraid.

GOVERNOR
Gentlemen, be careful and vigilant! All those sailors are armed!

ALL IN CHORUS
Yes, senior De Costa!

POLICEMAN
Go in quietly for sailors! Is it clear, for everyone what to do?

ALL IN CHORUS
Yes, sir!

POLICEMAN
Then, in you go, follow me! Shush?

He starts walking, but turns from side to side so as to look around. As one has not ended talking, when the Governor suspended the gesture to the Chief policeman.

GOVERNOR
Yes, I agree with Chief inspector, Gentlemen, you're had to be alert! These Naval officers are fully armed!

ALL IN CHORUS
Yes, senior Governor!

On the spot the Policeman joins in again, and is alleged.

POLICEMAN
We will get in tongue-tied? You're taken them all only alive! Is it understood?

ALL IN CHORUS
Yes, Mister Van De Bain!

REPORTER
Excuse me, Governor, what's the Commissioner intends…?

POLICEMAN
(Says to a policeman.)
Our police will have to put handcuffs on all of those seafarers hands!

PAUSE.

GOVERNOR
Then one makes a statement that they're arrested, According to our Laws. Is all clear? If not give a warning to open fire?

He talks is holding a notebook, and writes roughly in it.

———————◆━◆◆━◆———————

LIGHTS UP ON:

CARLOS

Winter's snow is circling, Round but forgot about love. White cold mold Heart of the void Clients. We feel been in Love, when the world is ruled by feints mirages. Winter mill chills blows by minus courage.

GORDON

In winter is cool, as has left the heart of agony. Soul is a fool, ruled - influences by bull. What we expect from love, Oyo, wei! Him not be an impotent? Winter chill fools, when settles in the heart, then feel it rules the world by unrequited Love? And what he waits from Love? Mug her as she can aid with no Soul?

WOMAN #2

As fans praise the song to the world for Love! But in response you only hear: it's feast, Carrots and peas...

(PAUSE.)

WOMAN #2

Then pain of separation. As men aid me, when is made to emancipation that leads to loneliness?

The police. Among them is the Police Chief. Next to him is the Governor in South America's region - Benito Machado. They're looking concerned and cautiously, trying to peek through the window inside the tavern "Tijuana".

The Chief Police gets hold of a gun Holster with a huge caliber, and cranks out his head from side-to-side.

Inn is illumination around to the Hall, that claiming outshone a group of these Policemen and the Governor.

As a result of that the Police Chief shoots.

When light has been turned off, they saw those Seamen.

POLICEMAN
(Says to a policeman.)
Too late to escape! They should remain in place, and throw their weapon on the floor! All of them need to lift their hand, then fold them over head! All get down to their knees!

REPORTER
All those seamen disappeared, Police Chief? But where did they all go?

- THE APOTHEOSIS OF THE SHOW.

The spectators see in the saloon are left standing only those girls that worked in there.

While on the floor remains lay dead Veronica - Paul, who's dressed in the sailor's uniform.

LIGHTS FADE.

EPILOGUE

PAUSE. The baby Matthew laughs, as waved his little hand towards the Sea waves.

From afar is a view of embarking in the port at Southern France "Jeannette", where on the upper deck seen that crew erect.

THE END.